A SUPERHERO TALE

Mark Dennion

**Cover illustration and logo design:
Ferdie Misa of Lungga Creatives**

DEDICATION

I was once told by a co-worker that every book needs a princess, so here is my princess: This book is for you, Kelsea Ryann Dennion! Daddy loves you!

Table of Contents

PROLOGUE

Prologue: (n) *a preliminary discourse; a preface or introductory part of a discourse, poem, or novel*

Most superhero stories start off with a mutated human chromosome or some sort of genetically engineered insect bite. This is a tale of superheroes, but it doesn't start that way.

The world has faced great peril a number of times.

Sometimes this peril has come from off-planet. If you don't believe, just ask a dinosaur (if you can find one).

Sometimes, the peril is homegrown. Many wars throughout human existence can attest to that.

But whenever these problems have arisen, the planet has had its own defense system to cope with them. After the extinction (or so we thought) of the dinosaurs, the planet marched on. Following every terrible war was a time of peace that at times led to future wars. Nevertheless, peace always prevailed in the end.

Now darkness was beginning to creep over the Earth -- a darkness that threatened to extinguish that prevailing peace.

In this time of impending peril, the world needed to find a way to defend itself once again. This time, the defense would come in the way of a few unlikely heroes.

CHAPTER ONE: The Human Dictionary

Dictionary: (n) *a book containing a selection of the words of a language, usually arranged alphabetically, giving information about their meanings, pronunciations, etymologies, inflected forms, etc., expressed in either the same or another language*

Richard was not the best student in the world. As a matter of fact, he was attending the university on a full athletic scholarship for martial arts. He had spent much of his youth training in a dojo and was one of the youngest black belts in the state. To maintain his scholarship, he needed to pull at least a "C" average. Every quiz, test, or term paper was of the utmost importance.

While studying *Sparknotes* for *The Great Gatsby* online in the stacks of the library, he stumbled upon a word that he was unsure of. His professor was a stickler for using vocabulary on quizzes, so he knew he needed to understand this word. Suddenly, an enormous thunderclap echoed over the building. Fearing he would lose electricity, Rich worked as fast as he could to get to Dictionary.com. The storm slowed the web browser, but it seemed to be loading fast enough. The home page of the site appeared. Rich quickly took control of the mouse and scrolled for the search engine. Just as he hit "Enter," a lightning bolt struck the computer server unit of the college, causing a massive explosion and energy surge. Rich was still attached to his computer when the surge hit it.

There was a sudden explosion on Rich's end, as well, and he was thrown from his chair. The explosion saved him from electrocution, but it didn't save him from everything. The moment the surge hit, Richard Shanary fused with the digital dictionary. An immense amount of data was electronically downloaded into his brain. No one would know it as they visited him in the hospital, but Rich was forever changed. He now had the superhuman ability of instant recall of any definition in the English language, and even a few in French, Spanish, Portuguese, and German.

Richard Shanary had become the Human Dictionary, a superhero bound to uphold the laws of society and grammar. His immense martial arts abilities and his power of instantly recalling the definition of the last word someone said to him were the perfect combination. He could distract someone with his new verbal ability and use his karate skills to finish the job!

Present Day

"All right, give me everything in your drawer and in the vault!" screamed a masked, armed assailant at a bank teller in the First Bank of Merchants. "Do it quickly and nobody gets hurt."

A crowd cowered in the corner. Many of them were crying, hoping that somehow they would survive this ordeal.

"Um, excuse me, sir, but the vault can only be opened by the branch manager," whimpered the cashier, "and he walked out on his lunch break a few minutes ago. He should be back in about twenty minutes. Can you wait?"

"Aw jeez, really?" said the perpetrator from behind his mask. "I got to pick my kid up from school in a half hour, but yeah, I guess so. But if I'm doing this, you had better get some more of these green lollipops out here right now!"

"Now! Adverb: at the present time or moment," someone said behind the criminal. A costumed character stood in the bank's doorway. "It seems to me that the only thing you need *now* is to feel the defining truth of justice!"

The crowded bank audience was hushed by the new arrival. The few children in the crowd giggled at the flashy costume.

"Jeez! Will you get a look at this clown?" said the crook, "I didn't know the circus was in town this week. My kid loves the circus."

The costumed man wore a navy blue unitard with yellow shorts pulled on over the spandex and a flowing gold cape over it all. His chest was emblazoned with a picture of an open book. Across the pages of the book the letters "HD"

He was aghast that someone would call him a clown! "Circus! Noun: a large public entertainment typically presented in one or more very large tents or in an indoor arena."

"Why do you keep doing that?" the crook asked, "Why do you keep repeating the last thing I say and then defining it?"

"It! Pronoun: used to represent an inanimate object previously mentioned."

"Stop that! It's really annoying!"

"Annoying! Adjective: causing annoyance," replied the caped crusader.

"Stop it!" yelled the crook. He approached the costumed hero and pointed his gun straight at him. "You're not going to be able to mimic me with an extra hole in your head. I don't have time for this. The crook glanced at his wristwatch. "Oh, jeez! My kid! Look at the time!"

"Time! Noun: the syst—"

"Stop it—" *BANG!*

In a rage, the criminal accidentally pulled the trigger. Unfortunately for him, he did it as he was still looking at his watch, causing him to shoot himself in the foot.

"Ouch!" the man screamed as he fell to the floor. The masked hero ran to the crook's side and kicked away the gun.

"Who... who are you?" asked the criminal as he lay dazed and confused.

"You! Pronoun: the pronoun of the second person singular or plural," replied the caped man. "As for me," he continued, "I'm the Human Dictionary!"

The would-be-robber rolled over and sank into unconsciousness. The crowd that was previously huddled in the corner advanced toward their hero, shouting his praises. They asked him many questions. His only reply was, "This is but one of the few defining moments you will see from me!"

Then suddenly, he disappeared out the revolving glass door and down the street, out of sight of the shocked crowd.

Word of the Human Dictionary soon spread. Many a criminal, low-life, and vagabond would soon be apprehended. They all made crucial mistakes out of frustration when they heard their last word repeated back to them and defined. In the extreme cases, the costumed hero used martial arts. There was no doubt about it: The Human Dictionary was cleaning and educating the streets.

But this sense of security would not last long. A dark shadow was creeping over the city. It was a dark shadow of crime and slang.

CHAPTER TWO: Thesaurus Rex

Thesaurus: (n) *a dictionary of synonyms and antonyms.*

Dr. Sinclair O'Nim, or Sin as his colleagues called him, was a man of science, and a man of words. For, you see, despite the doctor's immense knowledge of genetic and molecular sciences, he also suffered from acute forms of both obsessive-compulsive disorder (OCD) and autism spectrum disorder (ASD). In short, whenever the good doctor spoke, he seemed to always end his sentences with a series of synonyms for the last word he spoke.

This was the predominant tick associated with his OCD. He walked around all day speaking brilliantly, and then by day's end, he began to sound like the titular character from the movie *Rain Man*. Because he was challenged by these two disorders, he began working in the field of genetics and research. He hoped to one day alleviate or even end this daily battle. Unfortunately, Mother Nature would intercede before that.

In a remote desert somewhere in the United States. . .

Dr. O'Nim was one of a few elite scientists who were sanctioned to close a secret U.S. Army military base. The reason for such secrecy was because of the specific item the base contained: an unfossilized dinosaur egg. The government had planned to hatch the egg and use the beast inside as a sort of weapon. Unfortunately, a mega-million-dollar movie blockbuster beat them to the chase. The movie portrayed a dinosaur wreaking havoc on a heavily populated city, causing millions upon millions of dollars in damages. The government figured that the country was already in a recession and could not afford such a travesty to happen. The officials in charge ordered the destruction of the egg and the shutting down of the base. Dr. O'Nim was in charge of the shutdown.

On the last night of the base's existence, Sin sent home his team as he prepared to destroy the egg.

"Leave, exit, good-bye," Dr. O'Nim said to his crew. I'll finish up, wrap up, clean up." The crew left the doctor behind, relieved to go home. It was hard for Sin to watch the crew depart. It seemed as if his disability made it difficult for people to accept him in a social manner. Because of that, he never really had any friends. These people, who were locked in a remote military base with him, were the closest thing that he had ever had to friends.

Lonely, Sin turned back to his task. Moments before he euthanized the egg, a tremendous earthquake struck, covering the secret base with a landslide. Dr. O'Nim was severely wounded during the destruction. He knew that he could not hope for rescue. Since the base was supposed to be destroyed, no one would come inspect the site; even if they did, it would be too late for him.

Dr. O'Nim thought hard. He knew he had little time left until his own untimely demise. He was too weak to dig out, but the unhatched beast may not be. As a last-ditch effort, O'Nim decided to do something unprecedented. He would take a syringe filled with a serum he had been formulating with his own DNA and injected it into the dinosaur egg. This serum would mix his genes with those of the reptile's.

If it worked, he would be able to make a clone of himself -- a clone that was part him, but also part dinosaur! With any hope, he would be a man most of the time. And he would be a dinosaur whenever he needed it. He would be a monster, but he would be alive! In essence, he would be almost like the Incredible Hulk, only he would transform into a dinosaur instead of a muscular green-skinned humanoid. The problem was he did not have time to test his data. Hence, he had no idea what the real outcome would be.

The injured scientist navigated around the damaged laboratory as best he could, which was quickly running thin on oxygen. He bumped into fallen debris and caused himself more aches and pains. In the poor light that remained in the lab, he took the serum, a viscous green substance, and injected it into the egg. Then all became dark…

It could have been hours, or it could have been days, but Sin finally awoke. The first thing he saw was his human body dead on the floor in front of him. The serum must have worked!

He peered into a nearby reflection staring back at him was a twenty-foot green and blue monster. His experiment failed! He wasn't part man and part dinosaur -- he was all beast! Dr. O'Nim looked in horror and then attempted to cry in anguish. What came out was unexpected.

Instead of the voice of a horrible beast, Dr. O'Nim heard his own voice call out, "No! Nay! Never!"

The doctor was stunned.

He tried to speak again, but all that came out was an ear-splitting roar. The doctor could not understand.

In confusion he cried out again. This time, he heard his own voice. "Why? Motive? For What?"

His serum had worked, but it was flawed. It wasn't the result that he wanted. But it wasn't the failure he thought it was either. He'd merged his own insides with the dinosaur's outside.

He *was* a dinosaur.

Specifically, he was a Tyrannosaurus Rex -- albeit slightly smarter than your average prehistoric version. He could think with the same reasoning and intelligence as before, but he could only communicate in strings of similar words. Reasons for this scenario would have to wait. Nothing would matter if he didn't leave the avalanched base soon enough, as his oxygen supply was nearly exhausted.

It turned out the body of the megafauna was like a machine, maybe even better. It would have taken construction crews weeks to dig out the landslide, but thanks to his new claws and powerful tail, Dr. O'Nim accomplished it in mere minutes.

Now on the surface, Sin was able to see for the first time the true extent of Mother Nature's wrath. In all directions, there seemed to be nothing but destruction. The earthquake had destroyed the entire base. Nothing was left.

Suddenly, the now dinosaurian Sin heard something in the cool mountain air.

"Help," came a wispy voice.

The beast's superior hearing was picking up the sound of someone's distress call. Sinclair O'Nim, in his new beastly form, followed the cries until he came upon what looked like a side of the mountain with a roof on it. It did not take long for Sin to realize that a house had been crushed with someone trapped inside.

Sin began digging up the area. He came upon the wall to the house and ripped it off. Inside he saw a girl of about eleven or twelve with dark brown, curly hair. She was kneeling over an unconscious woman. With one look, the girl saw the monster and cried out in horror. Sin was taken aback by this. It took him several seconds to remember his new visage. He tried to calm the girl by speaking to her, but once again his terrible roar filled the nearby valley.

Dr. O'Nim stopped and thought. He realized he could only speak when he attempted strings of synonyms.

He collected his thoughts and tried to yell over the voice of the screaming girl. "Help! Aid! Assist!"

The girl stopped her screaming and looked at the behemoth. "What did you just say?"

Sin thought hard and once again heard his own voice. "Help! Aid! Assist!"

The girl didn't know how to react. Here was this beast, this dinosaur saying he was trying to help her. She didn't know if she was dreaming or in shock, but she nevertheless found herself responding to the monster. "My mom is hurt, and we need a doctor.

Sin knew that with his new "hands," he could offer no assistance. But he also knew that his new feet could.

He picked up the girl and hoisted her onto the back of his thick, scaly neck. Then he lifted up the woman.

The doctor-turned-dinosaur concentrated and tried to reveal his thoughts: "Hospital, clinic, infirmary," he started, and then changed to, "run, sprint, jog."

Crude as his communications were, the girl understood and held on tight. Minutes later they were outside an area emergency room. Sin dropped off the girl and her mother and ran off into the night.

The girl watched as he disappeared into the darkness. Then she ran inside and got help.

In the morning, local authorities and media stations were musing about the girl's sightings of a dinosaur who spoke in synonyms. Some of them thought the girl had dreamed it all in her panic. That was until they discovered a huge claw print just feet from where the woman and her daughter were found. Hours later, headlines broke out declaring there to be a "Thesaurus Rex" at large.

Unfortunately for Dr. O'Nim, there were no other large creatures in the area that could have made those tracks. Within a few hours, Thesaurus Rex was in a pair of elephant shackles and brought to justice. When he was taken into town, a crowd of people came out to gawk at him. Some of the onlookers screamed in horror that such a beast existed; others screamed that such a beast was being treated unfairly. Amid all the commotion, the young girl Thesaurus Rex had saved walked through the crowd and up to the monster.

The crowd quieted.

The little girl had so much she wanted to say to the beast. She wanted to tell him that her mother was fine because he'd saved her. She wanted to let him know how thankful she was that he responded to her cries of distress. She wanted to tell him how at first she was scared of him, but he helped show her that miracles and friends came in all sizes and shapes. But with the emotions that flooded through her at that moment, "Thank you" was all she could say.

She then wrapped her arms around one of the dinosaur's legs and hugged it. The crowd remained speechless, but Thesaurus Rex did not.

"Helper, assistant, friend!" cried Thesaurus Rex. The crowd began to stir. "Helper, assistant, friend!" he repeated.

And just like that, it was clear. This town was not cursed with an urban legend; rather, it was blessed with a friend. The sheriff broke the shackles and freed Thesaurus Rex, knowing that a time of justice, legality, and truth was just beginning.

14

CHAPTER THREE: Atlas

Atlas: *(n) a bound collection of maps.*

Sometime in the Past

By the age of seven, Michael Allen Philips could use a compass and a torn road atlas and could walk himself safely across the United States. As a matter of fact, he did do it -- twice! At that time it was estimated that if he continued at that pace, by the time he was twenty-five he would have every map in the world -- and maybe one or two from another planet -- memorized and could probably make adjustments to more than half of them.

It could almost be said that maps were in his blood. A walk around the Philips's estate would affirm that. The house was wall-to-wall maps. In the hallways, framed pictures of schematic maps decorated the view. In the study, topographic maps lined the walls. Political maps wrapped around the corners of the garage while physical maps were laid out in the utility room. The most unique part of the house had to be the library. The Philips's had maps of fantasy lands framed. One wall showed the land of *Narnia* flanked by the *Lonely Islands*. A picture of *Middle Earth* showed the borders of *Gondor* and *Mordor*. Other maps included *Oz*, *Neverland*, *Wonderland*, and even a place named *Naboombu*. They served no actual purpose, but they were maps.

Michael's father, Dr. Phillips, was a fourth-generation cartographer and the leading professor of cartography at City University. Michael's great grandfather was the first African American mapmaker for the United States Army during the First World War. Michael's father had high hopes that his son would follow in the family footsteps.

But adolescence hit Mike just like it hits most teenagers. Mike found it more important to hang out with friends and play video games than to study his maps. His skills began to dwindle. It became so bad that one day he stopped at a convenience store and asked for directions.

Despite his deficiencies and deteriorating skills, he was still better than most trained professionals at map making, reading, and editing. Because of this, it wasn't long after he graduated college before he was offered a professorship at City University which he gladly accepted. It was the perfect place for him to rest upon the laurels he worked so hard early on to make. He planned to just let his skills slip away until he could retire.

But this slide into map-reading ineptitude came to a screeching halt.

One cold October night, after teaching a class on geography at a local community college, Michael's father was struck and killed by a runaway truck. When the police questioned the driver, he claimed he didn't see the other car. He was lost and was preoccupied with unfolding a map when he veered too far across the line and hit Michael's father's car.

On that day, Michael Allen Philips vowed that no such event would ever happen again. He grabbed his father's torn satchel which carried all of the hard plastic cylinders filled with maps, and he ran.

Present Day

"I can't see anything in this fog," complained a woman behind the wheel as her toddler cried in the back seat. "Baby boy, just let mommy get to a gas station so I can get directions, and then I'll feed you, okay?"

The baby cried even louder, as if in protest.

The woman turned around to try and soothe the infant, but it seemed to no avail. When she turned back to the road again, a figure stood bathed in the headlights of her car. Instinctively, she slammed on the brakes.

"What are you doing in the middle of the road, you wacko?" the woman screamed at the figure.

The hooded figure approached. His face was concealed, but he carried a torn satchel over his left shoulder.

16

"I'm here to save your night," a throaty response echoed.

Fearing for her life and the life of her child, the woman began to rev her engine for a speedy escape. Suddenly, there was a quick movement from the shadowy figure followed by a loud pound on the hood of her car. The woman screamed.

When she looked out of her windshield, she saw the shadowy figure shining a light onto a sheet of paper.

"You see," the voice continued, "this road leads to absolutely nowhere. In about thirteen and a half miles, you'll hit a major highway, but the on-ramp is closed due to construction. It would have been another twenty-five miles after that before you would have found another intersection. And judging by the topographic layout of the terrain and that sound your car is making, I'm willing to bet that you don't have enough gas to make the trip."

Just then the woman looked down at her dashboard, and her yellow gas light flickered on. She stared in amazement at the figure in front of her.

"If you make a U-turn, you can be back on a major highway in less than two point three miles. Then you can feed your baby," the figure said.

Dumbfounded, the woman just looked at the figure. "Who are you?" she said.

The figure took a deep breath as if to signify a long upcoming soliloquy. "I am the living North Star; I am the compass rose to the lost traveler; I am the scourge of misdirection; I am Atlas!"

The woman, more in disbelief than shock, backed her car up, turned around, and drove away, leaving the hooded, satchel-toting figure shrouded in darkness. The figure waited until the lights of the car were no longer visible before he spoke.

"Wherever there is a traveler lost, wherever there isn't a gas station or convenience store, wherever a GPS is recalculating, I will be there. Be ready for some direction, world. Atlas has arrived."

CHAPTER FOUR: Lexi Con

Lexicon: *(n) the vocabulary of a particular language, field, social class, person, etc.*

Legends tell stories of twins. One born and destined to be good; the other bred for darkness and evil. One the Yin to the other's Yang, perpetually keeping balance in the universe. This story does not start out like that, but it may turn out that way in the end. Legend also tells of tales where twins, although separated by miles or even countries and continents, share a bond that is even stronger than nature. There have been stories of twins who finish each other's sentences while they sit in separate rooms, some who experience sympathetic pain for their womb mate, and even some who can practically read each other's mind. Ritchie and Lexi had never been those types of twins, but there was a first time for everything.

Present Day

A phone rang. Lexi rolled her eyes as she viewed the caller I.D. It was her slacker twin brother, Ritchie, who was off partying away a scholarship at some fancy college while she was stuck taking a few classes at a community college so that she could save money for graduate school one day. She picked up the call.

"What do you want, Ritchie?" she hissed into the phone.

"Whoa, what's with the venom, Lexi? I was just calling to say hi, and I miss you," replied the voice on the other end of the line. "Can't a brother do that?"

"No! No, a brother cannot because the last time that he did, I had to go convert some money into pesos for bail!" She sighed. "What is it this time? How much do you need?"

"I'm really hurt. You make it sound like I use you. I just know that I can trust you when it comes to my most vulnerable moments."

18

Lexi was taken aback. She never knew that was why her brother acted that way. She always thought he did things just to annoy her.

Choked up, she responded to her twin. "I'm sorry. Let me start over. Hi bro, what's up?"

"I need your help with a book report that's due tomorrow. Have you ever read *The Great Gatsby*?"

"You are such a jerk!" Her dark hazel eyes welled with anger. "I really fell for that vulnerable insecurity act. No, even if I had read *The Great Gatsby*, I wouldn't share one iota of information about it with you! Why don't you just take the easy way out and Sparknote it like you did all through high school? Then you could still have time to pass your classes, party away, and forget those who sacrificed so that you could be where you are today. Goodbye!" She hung up on him and tossed her phone on the couch.

How dare he do that to her! She was always the one on the losing side of the deck. Ritchie was the average student who gained a college scholarship because of his martial arts training. Lexi had to stay home. He got all the breaks. All she ever got was grief.

"Why can't you be more easy-going like your brother?" her parents would ask her when she was younger. "It's okay to get into some trouble now and then," they would continue. "You need to get out more!" The comments never stopped, and it was all because of Ritchie.

He never seemed to care about her, so why should she ever care about him? At times, she hated her brother. At times, she wanted to destroy him! She wanted to take away from him all that he took from her and keep it for herself.

Later that night, Lexi was microwaving a bag of popcorn in her small condo. She planned to eat it while watching *Skydiving with the Stars*, a new hit reality television show. Suddenly, she lurched forward in immense pain. Her head began to throb with an electrical sensation. She smelled something burning. Then came the rush. It was a one-two punch. First came the power -- the feeling of a new kind of strength that she never knew she had.

This feeling brought a happiness to Lexi that she hadn't felt in a long time. A smile began to spread. But then came the pain! It came in the form of a dull growing headache that matured itself into a full-blown migraine knocking on the door of an aneurism. As fast as it had come, the pain stopped, but the energy remained.

Power. That's what it was, Lexi thought. Pure, unadulterated power. Someone once said that knowledge was power. If that were true, then she was more powerful than the gods. The television continued to play in the background -- as if nothing out of the ordinary had happened. Lexi's ears pricked as the man on the screen explained the inner workings of a parachute to the next celebrity:

"At a certain point, you'll hit terminal velocity!"

As the man on screen said this, Lexi's mind flooded with information.

Terminal Velocity: (n) the velocity at which a falling body moves through a medium, as air, when the force of resistance of the medium is equal in magnitude and opposite in direction to the force of gravity.

Somehow, every word that she heard she was able to instantly define. She had no idea how this happened, but she knew now that everything had changed. She was no longer the little twin who got pushed around. She was no longer the bailout call. She was no longer the person to use. She was no longer Alexis Constance Shanary.

No, that girl was gone. All that remained was Lexi Con.

CHAPTER FIVE: Thesaurus Rex

Outside the Highway Commission Office

In his haste to inject the DNA serum that would genetically clone himself with a prehistoric beast, Dr. Sinclair O'Nim forgot to take into account the hunger. The beast that he had become craved sustenance all the time. The worst part of this constant demand for food was the selection. Dr. O'Nim maintained his own thoughts and memories during the cloning, but the rest of the brain, and body for that fact, belonged to the beast.

The things the doctor began craving made him sick, but Thesaurus Rex found them appetizing. The first time he stumbled upon a coyote in a field, he couldn't help himself from gorging on the animal. The residents who recently freed him began to fear for their pets. They did the next best thing to detaining him; they appeased him. An all-you-can-eat buffet.

Soon, he found himself feasting on a pile of roadkill outside the highway commission office. The smell of these rotting corpses made the doctor wince, but it made his mouth water.

As he feasted, he didn't notice the small shadow growing in front of him. When the shadow was fully formed, he looked up. It was the girl, the same girl he saved from the landslide and who later hugged him during his brief incarceration. With a flank of deer hanging from his jaw, he stared at the girl. Many people in this town looked at him as if he were some kind of bloodthirsty beast -- probably because he was one -- but not this girl. Here he was with half of Bambi hanging out of the side of his mouth (a scene that would horrify most adults, let alone children), and she was looking at him with an air of awe and wonder.

"Hello," she stammered.

Thesaurus Rex slurped down the limb like a strand of pasta. "Hello, welcome, salutations," he replied.

The girl giggled. "Why do you talk like that?"

Thesaurus Rex shrugged his beastly shoulders. "Uncertain, ambiguous, ambivalent."

"It's funny." She laughed. "I never really got to thank you. I mean, I did say thank you, but there was so much more that I wanted to say. A hug is really not enough reward for what you did. My mom is going to be all right. The doctors said another few minutes, and she would have…" she trailed off. "And that's the thing. Even with machines, no one would have been able to get to us in time to save us. So, thank you… ummm… dinosaur?"

Thesaurus Rex realized that she didn't really know who he was. But really, *he* didn't know who he was. He wasn't sure anymore if he could really be called a *who* rather than a *what*. He concentrated on his name and tried to speak it, but nothing happened. He tried again, but to no avail. It dawned on him that he couldn't say his name because there weren't any synonyms for it. His true identity, that of Sinclair O'Nim, would be forever trapped with his human body under tons of dirt from a landslide. He was no longer Dr. Sinclair O'Nim; he was Thesaurus Rex.

He decided that if he couldn't speak his name, he would describe himself. "Scientist, professor, doctor," he said. "Helper, assistant, friend."

"Dr. Friend?" the girl said. "I like that one. I'll call you Dr. Friend. I'm Ariel Adne, but you can call me Ari. Can you call me Ari?"

Thesaurus Rex shook his head side to side as if to signal "no."

"That's okay."

Ari sighed, and a saddened chagrin blossomed over her face. She looked deep into the beast's eyes and spoke. "I'm so happy that you were here to help me and Mom, but why haven't you left? Do you really like dead deer that much?"

Thesaurus Rex tilted his head in confusion.

"I mean, you were so helpful when I needed you. Other people could use your help too. There are so many more people that you could help in other areas than this small town."

Thesaurus Rex never thought of it like that. He had never thought about what he would do with this new life of his. He had to do more than to rid a town of its overgrowing population of roadkill.

"You see, my dad, he's the zookeeper in the city zoo," Ari went on. "I spoke with him. They could set you up with a nice home there. And they could feed you all day long without a problem."

Thesaurus was confused. "Specimen, sight, attraction?" he questioned.

Ari looked puzzled for a moment, and then she figured out the enigmatic clue. "No! No, nothing like that. Just a place to stay. You will be free to roam the city so you can help out. There must be thousands of ways you can help there. With the recent destruction of our house, my mom and I are moving back into the city so that family can help us out. And the best news is that I spend my weekends at the zoo helping my dad. I can visit you!"

Thesaurus didn't know what to think. He was never close to anyone before. Then one day he saved a girl's life, and the next thing he knew, he had his first friend. The thought of having someone care for him did feel right. And she brought up a great point. Since the landslide, there had been virtually nothing for him to do. The city was loaded with crime, strife, and other issues. Ari said it herself: he worked better and faster than any machine that humans had. He would have a purpose in life. Besides that, the idea of real food instead of roadkill did sound appetizing.

"Transaction, pact, deal!" the giant lizard said.

Ari squealed like a kid on Christmas. She began telling him of all the activities she had already thought of that they would do around the zoo. As the girl continued to speak, all the former doctor-turned-dinosaur could think was 'what have I gotten myself into?' He smiled.

CHAPTER SIX: Wu Slang Clan

Slang *(n): very informal usage in vocabulary*

The City

"And that was a defining moment," stated the Human Dictionary to the officer he had just helped apprehend a criminal.

"Please take me to jail," the assailant said. "Just get me away from that freak!"

"Freak. Noun: any person or animal on exhibition as an example of a strange deviation from nature; monster," replied the Human Dictionary.

"Stop it!" could be heard all the way down the block as the police car drove off.

"Thanks again, HD," commented a police officer as he approached his squad car "You really have a way of getting at those guys. This job has certainly become easier with you on the beat."

"No thanks needed, my good constable. My reward is a clean street, both physically and grammatically."

The two men parted company with the police officer making confused remarks under his breath.

***

On the way back to his apartment, the Human Dictionary overheard a police scanner (the blue light special he bought at Gadget Shack) relaying the message of a jewelry store heist.

"Suspects are at Dino's Diamonds on the corner of Westfield and Federal. Suspects are to be considered very dangerous."

"Dangerous! That is the definition of my job," the Human Dictionary said to himself. "Westfield and Federal. Wow, this time of day I could take 36ᵗʰ street, but I may get slowed down by a train crossing. I could always just take Maple."

24

"Both of those are terrible ideas!" a deep voice shouted from the shadows.

The Human Dictionary spun around on his heels into a fighting stance. An apron of steam parted in the shadows, and a dark, hooded figure walked forward. He was carrying a ripped knapsack and wearing a mask with what seemed like a crude globe painted over it. The figure whipped the knapsack off his shoulders and spun a rod-shaped object in his hands. Suddenly, he stopped, ripped open the object, and threw it on the ground, revealing a map.

"You see, you were right about the train. It should be arriving in a few moments. You would have lost close to a minute and a half sitting in train traffic." The figure's finger then looped around to the other side of the map. "You may not know this, but Maple is under construction. There are a few detours, but they will essentially lead you right back to 36ᵗʰ Street. Your best bet is to take Dudley. Topographically it is a nightmare -- loaded with hills -- but it has the least amount of obstacles in your way. Take this route and you will have an ETA of five minutes."

The Human Dictionary stood there wearing the confused façade of many of his own victims. "Ah, thanks…"

"Just call me Atlas," said the hooded figure as he slunk back into the shadows and out of sight.

"Weird," HD said to himself as he hurried down the prescribed route.

Five minutes later…

The Human Dictionary approached his destination with his calves screaming in pain. That Atlas guy wasn't kidding about all of the hills. As HD got closer to the jewelry store, he could see figures running, jumping, and flipping in and out of the broken plate glass window in the front of the store. He trudged forward toward the crowd of villains. In his most heroic pose, he introduced himself to the perpetrators.

"Halt, you minions of darkness," he called. Relinquish your booty now and surrender or feel the sting of justice and grammar."

Unsure of how to react, the robbers all stopped and looked at him. They all wore ridiculously large masks that not only failed to show a single facial feature but most likely obstructed their view at the same time. They began to point and laugh, commenting on his spandex tights, which was ironic because their costumes were far more ridiculous than his. Then they did something that completely threw off the Human Dictionary.

"Man, this fool be trippin'," the lead member said.

"Trippin'," stuttered the Human Dictionary. His mind raced, he began to get dizzy, his stance faltered, and he spread out his arms to steady himself. It was too late. The vertigo got the better of him, and he fell to one knee. "Trippin'. Informal language that does not have a definition. My -- my -- my powers are useless," HD noted to himself.

The gang members surrounded the fallen hero and continued to taunt him with their slang.

"Yo pops, this is triflin.'"

"What's the matter, homie?"

"Cat got your tongue, or are you just swoll?"

With each word spoken, the Human Dictionary felt weaker and weaker. He could feel his strength slipping away, and he was powerless to stop it.

"Yo, let's end this fool foreva," said one of the masked fiends. He then pulled out a gun and aimed it at the face of the powerless hero.

Just before the villain could pull the trigger, there was a flash of movement. Something swung down upon the gunman's arm, causing him to lose the weapon. The Human Dictionary caught sight of a knapsack full of maps just before it sent the gun flying.

"Why don't you leave the man alone?" Atlas queried. "It's obvious that your butchering of the English language is sickening him."

Leaving the Human Dictionary to suffer on the pavement, the members of the gang surrounded the new, map-wielding hero. They taunted Atlas with their slang; but when this did not have an effect on him, they poised themselves into unique fighting stances.

Atlas prepared himself for a fight as well. He was hoping that it would not come to that. Although he understood the principles of fighting, he had always been able to find his way out of confrontations without ever executing those principles. But it seemed that diplomacy was as lost on these boys as syntax and subject-verb agreement.

"Fool, I don't know where you came from, but in a second, you are going to wish you was back there," claimed the lead member.

Suddenly, from behind the gang came a loud booming voice. "There. Adverb: in or at that place," shouted the Human Dictionary.

With the gang's error of ending a sentence without a slang word, HD's instant recall rebooted him back to full strength. Before any of the gang members could react, the Human Dictionary was on them, and Atlas joined the fray. With a whirlwind of fists, elbows, and feet, the two heroes crushed any body part they could find. Despite years of formal martial arts training, the Human Dictionary had to admit these gang members were accomplished fighters in their own right.

The crowd started to disperse as a few members of the gang ran off. Atlas was locked in a fight with a minion while the Human Dictionary squared off with the gang leader. Suddenly, the two gang members made a whistling sound. As if on cue, they switched their fighting partners. The move worked in the villains' favor. The overmatched Atlas was knocked to the ground by the leader while the Human Dictionary was temporarily detained by the minion. HD promptly knocked his opponent unconscious. Then he turned his attention to the gang leader.

In classic form, the head gangbanger took off down the street, leaving a few of his unconscious minions in the hands of HD and Atlas. The Human Dictionary was determined to keep the scoundrel from getting away.

"Looks like it's time for a spell check!" exclaimed the Human Dictionary. He pulled from his side a small pouch. In it was an object in the shape of an elongated check mark. Engraved on the object were the letters "abc". HD pulled back his arm and slung the check at the running criminal. In a "batarang"-type fashion, the criminal was tripped up and fell a few yards from the hero.

While lying on the ground, the gang leader shuffled in his pockets and pulled out the same gun he threatened the Human Dictionary with earlier. HD dropped to the concrete and curled up to make himself into a smaller target.

Before the gang leader could fire, a sudden gust of wind blew the weapon out of his hand. With a mixed expression of fear and amazement, the unarmed gang leader regained his footing and took off down the street. As he ran, he shouted, "You best be believin' that you hasn't heard the last of the Wu Slang Clan!"

Now that the danger was over, HD returned to his fallen ally. He checked on Atlas and helped him up.

"Thanks for all the help tonight, citizen," said the Human Dictionary "I must admit that without you, I probably would be dead."

"Don't mention it; consider us even," Atlas replied. "I wouldn't have fared much better against those guys without you. By the way, nice throwing star. And how did you do the wind trick?"

"The throwing star was my spell check, a very useful tool, but you should never rely on it alone. The wind gust wasn't me. I don't know where that came from but thank the alphabet that it did. So, now that all of the excitement is over, how about you tell me the best way home; if possible, a way with the least amount of hills."

CHAPTER SEVEN: Lexi Con

A superhero, and therefore a supervillain, is only as recognizable as the costume that he or she wears -- it was Public Relations 101. Lexi Con knew this. She knew that to be recognized, and therefore feared, she needed a powerful costume.

In addition to a costume, she needed a suitable audience to be her test subjects for the uniform. The costume was the easy part -- it was amazing what you could buy on the Internet nowadays. The audience, however, presented a problem. Of course, this problem was as easily solved as the costume issue, thanks again to the Internet: the costume website advertised for this year's Comic Expo in the city convention hall. That meant thousands of people would be walking around in spandex and capes. Perfect!

Comic Expo

As hundreds of people walked the convention center floor, no one seemed to pay much attention to the woman wearing the purple and black cotton-polyester blend with the letters "LC" stitched on the chest. She stood in the center aisle with her hands on her hips, watching the spandex-clad crowd with disappointment. So far, this costume was a bust. Lexi Con soon realized that to get attention, she would have to start by drawing it to her. A pair of men dressed as space cadets from a popular television show began to walk past her. She called to them.

"You there! The twenty-eight-year-old who probably still lives with his mother. Come here!" she venomously spat at the passers-by.

Both men, who were as ridiculously dressed as Lexi, if not worse, stopped and stared at the red-headed woman in purple and black as if they weren't sure which one of them she was calling. Finally, they both approached her.

"You must have been talking to him," the one in the dark shirt said while pointing toward his friend in the white shirt, "because I don't live with my mom. I live in my dad's garage." He finished in a tone that seemed to be an attempt to impress her.

"Regardless, either of you will do," she noted. "What do you think of my costume?"

The two men stood there confused. Was this really the reason she had called them over?

The previously silent one was the first to speak. "Umm... who are you supposed to be? Is that the new Feline Female costume?"

"No, you moron, this is an original piece. Just tell me, do you feel that this is an outfit that will be remembered?"

The two men began to giggle. This was probably the first time, and definitely the last, that either of these men would ever be asked for fashion advice. They decided to play along.

"To be honest, you look a little... oh, what's the word I'm looking for...?" one of them questioned.

"Oh, let me help," the other chimed in with an air of sarcasm. "Could it be... 'pedestrian?'"

"That is exactly the word: pedestrian."

Lexi Con's mental recall kicked in immediately: pedestrian— adjective: lack of vitality, imagination, or distinction; commonplace. The realization set in that these two comic book researchers were calling her average. She boiled over with anger.

"As a matter of fact, if you were any more pedestrian, you would be a *muggle*," the dark-haired one finished.

Then it happened. Before Lexi Con could retaliate at the men for making fun of her, a blinding pain overcame her. Try as she might, she could not fix the word "muggle" to any definition. The pain became so intense that she nearly staggered to the ground. With every last bit of strength she possessed, she lunged at the man who spoke, grabbed him by the *Galaxy Wars* plastic ears he was wearing, and began to threaten him for information.

"What is a *muggle*?" she screamed at the man as she twisted his plastic ears. "What does it mean?"

"Look, lady, I'm really sorry! We were only messing with you. The costume looks great. Please don't hurt the ears. They're a collector's item."

"Never mind the insults, you penniless dweeb. What does *muggle* mean?" The white pain began to draw Lexi Con into a void; she could feel the world around her begin to slip away.

"Umm... non-magical person! Someone who is not a wizard!" he shouted.

Just like that, the pain went away. The white void dissolved, and once again Lexi Con could feel attached to the world. She released the man's ears and pushed him into his friend until they were both sprawled out on the floor and looking up at her.

This was the first time that such a feeling had ever come over her. It was like the night that the power had come to her, only more intense.

She looked at the boys, and a smile grew across her face. "Thank you for the compliments on the costume, boys. I'll remember them. And you should remember that I am Lexi Con." She paused for dramatic effect as she began to point her fingers all over her body, highlighting her costume. "I am the *definition* of evil," she declared. (And that is how her catch phrase was created).

"We'll do that," one of the men finally said, "and next time you need help with a definition, why don't you ask him?" He pointed to an autograph table where a costumed man was signing five-by-seven photos of himself.

"Who is that?" questioned Lexi Con.

"Who is that?" the men mimicked in response.

"Have you been living under a rock?" one continued.

"Or have you been living on an asteroid in the Garblax Nebula?" the other added.

Both men began to laugh at their own joke until Lexi Con froze them both with her icy stare. They each remembered how she had assaulted them over their last joke only moments before. They struggled to compose themselves.

The one with the partially torn rubber ears spoke. "That's the Human Dictionary. He has become a superhero, appearing all around the city to thwart evil. He took out some low-life criminal *and* some of the Wu Slang Clan just the other night. He has the amazing power of defining any word at will. Plus, I hear he is really good at karate."

Lexi Con stared at the spandex-clad figure with the wild hair sticking up above his mask. Although this was the first time she had ever seen him, she felt that she knew him. The broad shoulders, the square chin, the stupid smirk that just made her want to blame him for everything.

"Ritchie," she said to herself.

But how could he also define words? How was it possible that he shared her strange power? What had happened? It took her a minute or two before it dawned on her. The night of the blinding pain, the white numbness, and then the overwhelming sensation of the power flowing through her. Ritchie, her brother, was the reason. He was the reason for the pain. He was the reason for the numbness. He was the reason for the power!

That explains everything. That explains me! *But how, and why did he do this?*

She knew that all of these questions would be answered in time, but now she needed to go plan her next move. Rushing past the two men who still were sitting on the ground, she fled the convention hall. She knew when she got her powers that she needed to use them for a purpose. Now she understood what that purpose was. At last, she had the ability to destroy her brother!

"I think I'll finally take my parents' advice and get into some trouble," she remarked to herself as she fled.

32

CHAPTER EIGHT: Thesaurus Rex

The City Zoo

Living in a zoo was never on the "to-do" list for Dr. O'Nim. But to be completely honest, neither was cloning himself with a dinosaur. However, this move seemed to be one of the better things to happen to him since the cloning. Staying at the zoo was not going to be the difficult part; moving into the zoo was the real challenge.

Although the idea of a synonym-speaking dinosaur savior seemed to be well accepted by the people who lived just outside the city near the country road, officials believed that such news would not be as well received by the people who lived in the metropolis. Because of this, the zoo sent a large truck with a trailer, usually used to transport larger animals such as rhinoceroses and giraffes, to pick up Thesaurus Rex.

Apparently, Ari spoke too soon when she mentioned that he would have free reign of the city streets. The mayor and the chief of police would not mind letting him roam on a probationary period, but only at night when he couldn't scare the general population. They wanted the city folk to warm up slowly to the recently un-extinct monster. To parade him down the main street when he first arrived seemed like a bad idea, especially since Thesaurus Rex already "voiced" concern about being a sideshow attraction. But still, his move to the city brought him closer to a life with meaning and closer to Ari.

Thesaurus Rex hoped his accommodations at the zoo would be slightly roomier and far less aromatic than the transport vehicle.

As the truck finally pulled up to the cargo bay at the zoo, a sense of relief washed over Thesaurus Rex.

"Hub, base, home," he said to himself.

After he exited the back of the trailer and stretched his legs, he saw a middle-aged, brown- haired man approach him. The man had a full beard and mustache and wore a green polo shirt with the

33

zoo's logo emblazoned on the lapel. He walked with a brown-haired girl in tow; it was Ari.

"Hi, Dr. Friend," she shouted to the monster as she rushed over and hugged his huge scaly thigh.

The older gentleman stood to the side with a little trepidation and watched the event. After his daughter released her strangle hold, he approached the dinosaur.

"Hello, umm... Thesaurus Rex. I am Dr. Roger Adne, Ariel's father and head zookeeper. I believe that I have a lot to thank you for. Without your help, I would not have my beautiful daughter with me today. There is no amount of thanks or favors that I can do to truly express my gratitude to you."

Dr. Adne was very uncomfortable. For starters, he was talking to something that he had been taught since he was a child had been extinct for millions of years. Worse than that, he was expecting it to respond to him. The most mind-blowing detail was the strange friendship that his daughter had developed with this creature.

"Stop, cease, desist," replied the gargantuan reptile. "Favor, aid, gift."

The zookeeper looked even more puzzled than before, if that were possible.

"He's saying that he did it as a favor, and you don't need to repay him at all, Daddy," Ari said.

"Be that as it may, I just hope that staying here is a little more comfortable for him than that highway patrol station you were talking about."

Dr. Adne walked them over to an open holding pen. "Sorry about this. We are renovating one of the old pachyderm corrals for you, but until it's done, this is all I have for you.

Thesaurus Rex looked at his temporary home. Up until now, he had been living on the side of a dusty highway road. The holding pen looked like a Four Seasons to him. Dr. Adne could tell from the beast's body language that this was a suitable arrangement.

"Come, let us get you something to eat," the zookeeper said. "How do you feel about seeker deer meat?"

The doctor's mind went to thoughts of disgusting entrails and bones, but the monster's mouth began to salivate.

"Sounds like you guys are about to do some really disgusting stuff," Ari remarked, wrinkling her nose. "I'm going to check on the tortoises to see if they moved from the last time I saw them… and the time before that… and the time before that."

Laughing, Dr. Adne replied, "Okay honey, but stay out of trouble."

Ari waved to the two doctors as they watched her retreat out of sight -- and closer to danger than she had ever been before.

The other side of the zoo…

Animals have uncanny senses that humans cannot even imagine. What happens when you import a millennia-old predator into an area of caged and frightened creatures? The animals can sense a danger they have never known but their ancient ancestors perished from.

In the new pachyderm exhibit, Tusks the African bull elephant sensed a new danger. It was a perceived threat he had never met before, but he knew to fear for his life. This caused him to rampage.

The bull charged at the walls of his habitat, quickly scaled the small barriers, and trampled the zoo promenade located directly outside his exhibit in an attempt to escape this new fear. Children and adults began screaming and running in different directions. Zoo security reacted immediately, but a group of unarmed men in golf carts were no match for a raging elephant.

The elephant continued him rampage down the zoo's main thoroughfare. The assault brought him to the reptile house. Standing directly in front of it was a young girl in a yellow tank top, blue jean shorts, and a purple hair tie.

The zoo holding pen…

Dr. Adne could hear the screams of people erupting all over the zoo. He grabbed a nearby two-way radio and searched for answers for all of the commotion.

"Dr. Adne," a voice chimed in over a shower of static, "Tusks, the bull elephant, is rampaging on the other side of the zoo. He is heading right for the reptile house!"

Dr. Adne allowed the news to sink in for a mere second before he took off running toward the scene, screaming, "Ariel!"

He made it not more than a few yards when he was overtaken by a large blue-green blur as Thesaurus Rex ran past him to the aid of his only friend.

On the other side of the zoo…

Ari was speaking to the tortoises, trying to coax them into moving just a few inches. She feared they might actually be dead because she had never seen them move. Suddenly, there was an explosion of noise to her left. When she looked up, hundreds of people were running straight at her -- along with one very large elephant.

Ari was so terrified that she couldn't move. She finally understood how the tortoises must have felt. The elephant moved closer until Ari could smell the odor of wet hay on the beast's breath. She closed her eyes as tight as she could and waited for it all to end. Suddenly, a loud roar drowned out all the other sounds.

Thesaurus Rex ran up upon the elephant and slammed his whole body into the large animal's side. The pachyderm stumbled and fell sideways into the big statue of a dinosaur located outside the reptile house.

The living dinosaur turned toward his friend and spoke. "Protection, asylum, safety!" Ari immediately came out of her motionless trance. She turned to run and saw her father rushing toward her.

Meanwhile, Tusks the elephant regained his footing and realized he was staring at the source of the immense fear he had never felt before. His natural instincts took over. If something is challenging your superiority in the jungle, you smash it to prove you are its better. He knew that was what he must do. He charged tusks first at the beast in front of him.

36

Once Thesaurus Rex realized that Ari was out of danger, he turned his attention back to the bull elephant. Had he turned a few seconds later, it would have been the last thing he'd ever done.

The elephant slammed into the dinosaur and pushed him backwards. The pachyderm's razor-sharp tusks narrowly avoided the giant reptile's sternum but grazed his short right arm instead. A trickle of blood began to pool on Thesaurus Rex's injured forelimb before running down his claws and dripping to the ground. The force of the impact caused the dinosaur to fall to the ground. A tremor shook the entire zoo and was felt several blocks away.

The elephant continued to try to gore his reptilian opponent. Thesaurus Rex quickly regained his footing and grabbed the charging mammal's head. He was able to turn the elephant around so that it was no longer pushing the giant into the throng of zookeepers behind them. Despite the overwhelming limitless possibilities of this new body, Dr. O'Nim's mind knew that it was completely untested. He didn't know how long he would be able to keep up such a skirmish.

As the beasts fought, an army of zookeepers and security guards formed ranks behind Dr. Adne and Ari.

"Daddy, you have to help Dr. Friend" Ari shouted. "He's hurt. Look! His arm is bleeding!"

"I know, honey," Dr. Adne said as he turned his attention to one of the zookeepers. "How are we coming on that tranquilizer gun?"

"We have one ready sir, but the problem is the animal's heart rate," the animal warden replied. "If we overestimate how fast its heart is beating, we could kill it. If we underestimate, it will have little to no effect."

"What about all the other lives at stake? Not just the animal's?"

"The only other life in danger is that monster you brought here. All other people have been evacuated from the area."

Dr. Adne looked at the zookeeper, and a thought blossomed in the doctor's head. "The monster that I brought here... call up the holding pen on the two-way. Tell them I need a ride!"

The two titanic combatants brought their battle to the walls of the reptile house. Thesaurus Rex was able to drive the large gray animal's skull into the concrete wall in an attempt to knock him unconscious, but the elephant's head was very hard. The dinosaur only succeeded in opening a small laceration between the eyes, thus angering him even more.

The elephant gained position on the dinosaur and once again was able to throw him to the ground. The pachyderm sized up the dinosaur to try and drive his tusks right through his foe's torso.

Ari screamed in horror at the sight. She was watching her friend about to be killed, and all she could think about was that she brought him here.

Just then, behind the battling giant, the same truck and trailer that brought Thesaurus Rex to the zoo backed up near the battle with Dr. Adne behind the wheel. As he lay on the ground, Thesaurus Rex could hear the machine pulling up. The irritating beeping sound was loud enough for anyone to hear, let alone someone with advanced reptilian hearing.

An idea came to Dr. O'Nim just as the elephant tried to run him through. As the big gray mammal charged, Thesaurus Rex braced his back against the cement sidewalk and thrust his legs into the bulk of the beast. The impact caused the pachyderm to stumble backward and into the open trailer which pulled up behind it.

The enraged beast was not deterred for long. He immediately gained his footing and prepared to charge again. A number of zookeepers ran toward the trailer door in an attempt to close it, but it was clear that their efforts were useless.

Suddenly, a very small but powerful gust of wind ripped through the zoo. It flew as if it had a purpose, avoiding contact with everything except the trailer door. The door violently slammed shut and latched closed before the elephant could reach the entryway. The raging Tusks was caged once more.

"Quickly!" shouted Dr. Adne. "Get that rig as far away from here as you can and away from any civilians. Get that mammoth to calm down. Tranq it if you have to."

Thesaurus Rex lay on the ground of the zoo right outside the reptile hut. The statue of one of his predecessors stared down on him. Thesaurus Rex looked at it and could sense an air of pride coming from it.

In his first true test, Thesaurus Rex had "passed, succeeded, achieved." He lay there gathering his strength and was deluged with a torrent of hugs from Ari and a tireless accompaniment of thanks and bandages from Dr. Adne.

CHAPTER NINE: Atlas

In a City Gym

Training.

He needed more training.

After the encounter with that inner city karate gang, the Wu Slang Clan, Atlas realized that a lifetime of no formal fight training had become a hindrance in his plan to save the city's lost patrons.

The fight put his superhero career into perspective. It showed that the bad guys had moves; that the Human Dictionary could hold his own. It had to be HD's moves that brought up the media hype around him. HD was given most of the credit for the arrest of a few of the Wu Slang members. Atlas was only a footnote in the story. If he had had more formal training, maybe it would have been he instead of the Human Dictionary that was invited to be a guest speaker at Comic Expo.

But when it came to fighting, Atlas was completely lost. The irony of that sank in -- he was the best map reader/writer/translator in the world, yet for the first time in his life, he felt completely lost. Years of living with generations of cartographers, and he had no idea where to go from there.

Wait. Yes, he did. He was drawing the new map of his life right now. He had signed up for fighting classes. With the instruction that he was going to learn, he would become more of a fighter and less of a liability.

The master of the lesson entered the room and approached the gathered group, hungrily waiting for instruction. Michael Allen Phillips was prepared for his introduction into the world of fighting.

"Okay," began the instructor. She scanned the area of the makeshift workout room converted from an old racquetball court. "Welcome ladies," she began as her eyes fell upon Mike, "-- and gentleman -- to Self-Defense for Beginners. Tonight we are going to teach you how to protect yourself, if the need arises. Let's begin."

She invited the group -- seven women and Mike -- to spread out and begin with some stretches. Of course, Mike felt a slight sting of embarrassment, but he knew that it would be better to be embarrassed here than out on the streets in a fight.

After a few basic stretches and calisthenics, the instructor began the first lesson in self-defense.

"Okay, ladies... I'm sorry, *and* gentleman... I'm so used to having a class of only ladies. I apologize again for the slip-up. Let's begin with the most basic moves. Sir," she said as she pointed to Mike, "how about you come forward and volunteer to help me show everyone else the basic moves?"

Mike thought this was a perfect idea. What better way to get exposure than with a little hands-on experience. He walked up to the instructor and awaited directions.

"Excellent! Why don't you stand directly behind me," she directed.

"Should I assume some sort of fighting stance?" he asked.

"No, just take the position behind me."

He did as he was told. It sounded cheesy, but he could already feel himself becoming a better fighter.

"Okay, now, ladies, when placed in a situation where self-defense is needed, it is best to think of a SIGN."

After saying this, she quickly turned and began to pummel Mike. Seconds later, he was lying on the floor and gasping for breath. He felt she had done more damage to him than the Wu Slang Clan had.

"Thank you for volunteering, sir. Now, ladies, did you understand what I meant by SIGN?" she asked as she helped Mike to his feet. "SIGN is an acronym that identifies the four most vulnerable spots where you can assault an attacker." Seconds after the instructor assisted Mike back to his feet, she began to pummel him again.

"First, 'S' is for sternum," she said as she lowered a sharp elbow into Mike's, instantly knocking the wind out of him. "Next, 'I' is for instep," she remarked as she brought her heel down on

Mike's foot. Mike began to hop around on one foot as he gasped for breath. "The third step, ladies, is the bread and butter. 'G' stands for groin!" she happily announced as she thrust a fist in Mike's nether regions, causing him to double over in excruciating pain.

Tears began to well in his eyes.

"And finally, 'N' stands for nose. Now, if you have successfully completed the first three steps, it should be sticking out like a target for you, much like our volunteer's is."

She wound up and kicked Mike square in the nose. The momentum of the blow caused him to fly backward and land flat on his back.

Sprawled out on the floor, Mike began to think, *Maybe this* is *more embarrassing than being out on the streets.*

"Let's have a nice big round of applause for our volunteer, ladies. What do you say?"

The group began a low roar of applause for the battered volunteer.

"Now," continued the instructor, "are there any questions?"

She scanned the crowd once again. The women of the class seemed satisfied with the directions given. Then she spotted her recent victim with his hand in the air.

"Yes, sir? How can I help you?"

"These tactics are all well and good," he said between heavy gasps for air, as he was still recovering from the initial blow of the onslaught, "but how do we defend ourselves in a more insecure environment? What I mean is, how can we defend ourselves against... oh, I don't know... a group of slang-speaking ninjas?"

The instructor held her sides as she laughed. She composed herself before answering her student's question.

"Why would you be fighting a group of slang-speaking ninjas? This class is to teach women walking home from work a few moves from professionals to disable an attacker so they can then run for help. This isn't a class for vigilante fighting instruction."

While the rest of the class laughed, Mike came to the conclusion that his last epiphany was correct: it would be less embarrassing on the streets.

"Tell you what," continued the instructor, "if you are walking home from work one day, and you are confronted by a gang of slang-speaking ninjas or country western-twanging samurais, this is what you do. Disable your attacker, run to the busiest street corner, then at the top of your lungs call for the Human Dictionary. He should be able to help you." The instructor laughed. "And if he isn't available, you can call on his sidekick, punching bag Atlas." The woman finished that sentence in a fit of hysterics.

Great. In less than ten minutes he had been beaten up by a girl and been called a sidekick punching bag. It was time to call it a night.

The ladies composed themselves from their frantic laughter and began to partner up to practice the new self-defense moves they had just learned.

Mike used his advanced skills and found the quickest way out of the old racquetball court and headed toward the men's locker room where his hoodie and satchel of maps awaited him.

CHAPTER TEN: The Human Dictionary

In an area music store

Training...

He needed more training.

After his run-in with the nefarious Wu Slang Clan, the Human Dictionary came to the realization that he had flaws. The least of which was the fact that, despite years of martial arts training, he needed to get back into shape (those hills were killer). But most important, HD had discovered his kryptonite.

All of the great heroes of the past had some sort of weakness. To the impenetrable Superman, the rock kryptonite robbed him of all his powers. To the boy wizard Harry Potter, it was the presence of his arch enemy. To the Human Dictionary, it was slang! It seemed that whenever one of those gang members spoke an informal word, HD was rendered powerless. What was worse was that it seemed that his powers now had a direct link to his physical strength! So, whenever slang was spoken, he went from hero to liability. He needed to train to somehow counter this effect. That was why he was here.

Richard Shanary, the secret identity of the Human Dictionary, stood in the middle of a popular music store among aisles of compact discs, absorbing song lyrics. The chorus of a twangy country western song echoed through the shop:

"With my whiskey in my hand
And an apple-peeler in my shoe,
Been bamboozled by my own hoss
I'm tired of his ballyhoo."

His brain began to tingle. Try as he may, Rich could not find the meaning of either "hoss" or "ballyhoo." Thankfully, the song died away. So did the neutralizing sensation in his brain.

44

The room began to shake as the bass of a popular hip-hop song boomed over the store's speakers. Every time an informal word was spoken, the sense of vertigo overcame the Human Dictionary. After a while, a dull white numbing sensation would come over him as if he were suffering from a migraine. The effect would not last long. The lyrics ran by so fast that Rich was able to pick up on a few formal words in between the harsh tribal beat of the song, and he would momentarily regain strength.

But the damage was visible. Rich entered the store a spry young man in his twenties. Moments later he looked physically ill and seemed disoriented. It was not long before a salesperson was bugging him.

"Can I help you?" asked a young woman wearing a polo shirt with the store's insignia embossed onto it.

Richard struggled to concentrate on her words, relying on them for strength. He was also distracted by the young woman's beauty. Strange as it may seem, spending his nights on the streets trying to clean up the community and their language and grammar, left little time for a social life. This sales girl was striking, and her presence had temporarily distracted him from the migraine-producing hip-hop lyrics.

"I'm all right," he replied. "I'm just browsing."

"'All right' may not be the term you're looking for. You look like you're in immense pain."

Rich thought for a minute. This was foolish. He couldn't betray himself in public by continuing to enter music stores and almost needing to be wheeled out of them on a stretcher. He needed to purchase one of these compact discs and return to more trusting surroundings.

So, he decided to lie his way out of this one. "No, I'm not in pain; I just have severe seasonal allergies. But thank you for your concern… uh…"

The girl fixed the backward name tag that was dangling on a lanyard around her neck.

"Abigail," she said. "Sorry about that. This stupid thing is always spinning around. One time a customer actually thought my name was 'Ask me about Surround Sound'. My name is Abigail."

Cute name for a cute girl, Rich thought.

"Thank you, Abigail. How much is the compact disc that is playing right now?" He wriggled his eyebrows flirtatiously as he asked this.

"Really? You look too preppie to be into the death gangsta rap. To each his own. It's regularly priced at $17.99, but it's on sale at 15% off. If you sign up for our distinguished shopper's card, you get an additional 10% off your purchase."

"So, I get 25% off if I sign up for this card?"

"Not really. That is a common misconception. You get the 10% off the already reduced 15% price. It comes to about 23.5% off the original price."

"My apologies."

"In addition, there is also a five dollar mail-in rebate. So, when all is said and done, if you sign up for a distinguished shopper's card, your grand total would be $8.76."

Shocked, Richard Shanary looked at the young woman. "That was a pretty impressive trick. Do they have you memorize all of those sales prices?"

"No, that's just me. Math has always been easy for me. I can do long division in my head better than most math teachers can do it on paper. Numbers are my thing. But when it comes to words, I'm a complete idiot. I once had a test that asked the question 'What is a pronoun?' I answered, 'A noun that gets paid.' Words I don't get; numbers make sense to me."

Richard looked admiringly at this girl. "Don't give up on words. Words were once my Achilles' heel too, but now I guess you could say they are my superpower," he joked with her.

"Yeah. Maybe one day I can become a superhero with my math abilities, like that Human Dictionary guy, or maybe Atlas. Or, maybe even that dinosaur thing down at the zoo that wrestled that elephant."

Richard thought to himself that maybe in another lifetime -- one where he wasn't so busy cleaning up the streets and their grammar -- he would actually have liked to ask this girl on a date. A lot would have to change before that could happen, though.

"Well, I wouldn't go that far. Those people put their lives at risk by doing what they do, but you could have a future in a math field still. Look at today. Your powers have rendered me helpless. I have no other choice but to be able to save --"

"48.69%," she interrupted.

"48.69% it is. Now where is the register?"

"Right this way," she said with a smile.

Abigail escorted Rich to the register to finalize his purchase.

Little did Rich know that his performance inside the music store was being closely watched, his demise carefully planned.

CHAPTER ELEVEN: Magazine and Clip(ping)

Periodical: *(n) a magazine or other journal that is issued at regularly recurring intervals.*

In the same mall as the music store…

Lexi Con stood surreptitiously in the mall walkway opposite the music store. She was keeping a close eye on her brother. She knew that to be able to finally bring an end to Ritchie and the Human Dictionary, she would have to know both of them inside and out. She stood in front of the comic book store just watching and remembering all that she saw.

At first she could sense something was wrong with him. Before he entered the store, he was his usual stoic self. But now he looked ill and confused. Just when he began to look his worst, he started flirting with the salesgirl. That brought some color back into his cheeks.

But something got to him in there. The only evidence she had to work with was the booming bass line of a song being pumped out of the store's speakers. This was powerful information; all she needed to do was to learn how to use it.

His conversation with the salesgirl added no new information except that he was a terrible flirt. She decided that she had seen enough for the day and left. As she rejoined the flow of foot traffic in the mall, she slammed into a man walking out of the comic book store. The man fell to the ground. A friend of his walked up next to him and began to chuckle at his fallen comrade.

"Why don't you watch where you're walking?" she snarled at the man sitting on the ground.

The man held his brown paper bag with the treasures he had purchased at the comic store and shouted back a snide remark at the woman. "Watch where I'm walking? How about you open your eyes. You're the one who entered the flow of traf—"

The man stopped speaking as he looked at Lexi. His jaw dropped as he pointed at her. "It's you!"

Lexi was not one for public recognition, at least not while out of costume. She began to blush and started to walk past the two gentlemen. The man sitting on the ground quickly got to his feet and cut off her path while dragging his other friend.

"Look, Josh!" the man shouted. "It's her, the cotton-polyester blend girl from Comic Expo. We have been looking everywhere for you!"

Lexi peered into the man's eyes and remembered that day. She recalled assaulting this man (and his plastic ears) for information. After she bled all of the information she could out of him, she threw him and his friend to the ground and left them behind.

Lexi began to smile. Her costume and first public impression had been memorable enough that she was recognized out of costume.

"Keep your voice down if you treasure your real ears as much as you treasured those plastic ones," she said between gritted teeth. "Why were you searching for me?"

The two men began to giggle again. They looked like two kids at Christmas who were told to open the *big* box in the corner.

She raised her eyebrows as a gesture stating "talk or be harmed."

"Well, the thing is, we were highly impressed by your performance at Comic Expo."

The news took Lexi aback. This was not what she expected to hear.

Suddenly, behind the two men-children, Lexi saw a figure approaching. Ritchie was walking through the mall, carrying his Music World shopping bag. To avoid detection, Lexi reached in and hugged both men very tightly in an attempt to cover her own face. The giggles persisted until she threatened them again. She pushed them apart when she figured Ritchie was far enough away.

"So, you were impressed, and you wanted to hunt me down and tell me this?" she questioned.

49

"No, not exactly. We have ulterior motives."

Lexi stared at them, waiting for an explanation. "Are you going to tell me, or is this a game? Is there a hidden camera somewhere?"

"Sorry, I just don't have much experience speaking with girls," the one named Josh replied. "We wanted to ask if we could join you."

"Join me?"

"Yes, like we could be your henchmen," his friend added.

Lexi looked over the two men. "You raise a good point, that a villain such as me should be accompanied by astute henchmen. But why would I choose you two?"

"We'll show you," they answered in unison.

At a firing range on the outskirts of the city...

The thunder of the gunfire echoed in the valley as the two men finished firing at their respective targets. Lexi looked in amazement at each bullseye circle. Both targets had been completely shot out from over fifty feet away!

"How did you two become so good at this?" she asked.

"Look at us," Josh replied. "We have spent way too many hours playing video games. It really developed our hand-eye coordination and aim."

"Impressive. Where did you get the guns?"

"Oh, they are completely legal. We bought them at gun shops and have the proper licenses."

Lexi looked at them and mumbled something under her breath about criminals that followed the law. "Exactly why do you want to help me anyway?"

"All our lives we have grown up idolizing the comic heroes who save the twerps like us. And do you know what happens after the hero saves the twerp? Nothing! You never see the twerp and the hero going out for pizza on a slow night, or even catching a movie together. And the worst of it all is that the hero usually runs off with the girl the twerp is fawning over. It's time that this stops. It's time for the twerp to be recognized!"

"Clearly you have deep-rooted psychological issues, which makes you more qualified than ever to assist me," Lexi lamented.

"You mean we have the jobs?" non-Josh asked.

"To be good henchmen you need to have some sort of title. I just can't be calling you Josh and... what is your name?"

"Heathcliff," the other man replied.

"I probably would have left my name anonymous as well," Lexi said, "but I can't call you Josh and Heathcliff now, can I?"

Josh and Heathcliff looked at each other with big smiles and began giggling again.

"Is there something I should know?"

"We have put a lot of thought into this," Josh said, "We figured as an homage to our most favorite gun-toting superhero, we want to be called *The Retaliators!*"

"Absolutely not. For one, you just gave me this whole soliloquy of how much you hate superheroes. Now you want to pay homage to one? No."

"I was prepared for this," Heathcliff chimed in. "I respect your whole school-related theme. I thought that maybe you could call me *Magazine*. You see, it's a periodical and gun cartridge, so it has that whole double meaning going for it."

"That's acceptable."

"Oh, and I have a good one. You can call me *Clipping* because that is a part of a newspaper and another name for a gun cartridge. And you can call us *The Periodicals!*"

"Clip is another name for a gun cartridge, not clipping, you moron," Magazine chided.

"Enough! You two give me a worse headache than hip-hop music. Magazine and Clip(ping), you are officially my henchmen. You will do my eternal bidding and never once complain or get paid. Agreed?"

"Agreed," the Periodicals responded.

"Excellent! Now that I have some help, here is my plan to take down the Human Dictionary..."

CHAPTER TWELVE: Thesaurus Rex

The City Zoo

"Well, that should do it," Dr. Adne said as he finished wrapping the superficial wound on Thesaurus Rex's arm. "Your skin is amazing! A fully-grown bull elephant like Tusks can charge with over a hundred thousand pounds of pressure per square inch, and he barely cut you open. I have had paper cuts worse than this. Your skin is essentially bullet-proof!"

Thesaurus Rex didn't even care about the flesh wound. All he cared was that his heart was all right. And his heart stood to the left of him, gently stroking his uninjured arm. Ari was his heart.

"Well, these events have certainly put a damper on our housing plans for you. The enclosure that we are creating for you is far enough away from the general population of the zoo that it should not cause any more problems like today, but the holding pen we were going to keep you in is much too close. This means that we are going to have to temporarily keep you in the quarantine area on the other side of the zoo. It is far enough away from the rest of the animals. Unfortunately, it is also considerably smaller than the regular holding pen."

Thesaurus Rex looked anxiously at the doctor. Although Rex was small in comparison to many other dinosaurs (a genetic defect that may have happened during the gene cloning sequence), he was still considerably larger than most zoo animals. He knew that he would need space to stretch his legs.

Before he could voice these concerns in a string of synonyms, Dr. Adne belayed his fears. "I know what you're going to say. I have spoken with both the mayor and the chief of police. They have reviewed your track record -- including the event with Tusks -- and they don't see why you wouldn't be able to roam the city to stretch your legs. They only ask that we alert them at the times that you will be going out, and that you do it at night. They still fear what the public would think if they saw a large dinosaur strolling around the streets without warning.

"Tonight, this evening, after dark," Thesaurus Rex spouted.

"Okay," Dr. Adne said. "I'll contact the authorities. Just try not to make a spectacle of yourself."

The City streets, later that evening...

Freedom. Although he knew he wasn't a prisoner, at times Thesaurus Rex felt like one. His evening constitutional was all he needed to reassure himself that he had made the right decision in coming to the city. He strolled up and down city boulevards, being especially careful to tread on the city streets rather than the soft ground. He'd been advised not to leave behind any tracks.

While he walked, he saw wonders he never thought he would see. Years of being stuck in a laboratory had robbed him of the pleasure of taking in the sites of the city: towering skylines, beautiful murals, and the historic part that many people today take for granted. All of this was his to admire.

Suddenly, his keen sense of hearing picked up a commotion. He tried to focus in on the source of the sound, but the city's skyline made cavernous walls. Sounds bounced and echoed all around, making it nearly impossible to determine the direction of the source. Then a small wisp of a wind blew up, carrying with it an unusual scent: the smell of gun powder. Using his keen sense of smell, Thesaurus Rex honed in on the source, following it until he found the commotion that he heard just moments before.

The sight he beheld both amazed and horrified him. The saurian hero watched while a group of hooded men yelled slang-laden remarks at a caped figure who was cowering on the ground. Then they attacked the man who lay helplessly on the ground.

Thesaurus Rex was unsure of what to do. He knew what was going on was not supposed to be happening, but at the same time, he knew of a new group of vigilante superheroes who were roaming the streets at night. What if the group of men attacking were these heroes? He didn't want to intercede and stop them from doing their jobs. Then he heard something that completely changed his outlook on the situation.

"Yo, I'm done with this fool!" cried one of the hooded men. "Let's do what we should had done before: waste him and split!"

Thesaurus Rex may have, at one time, been Dr. Sinclair O'Nim, world-renowned scientist, but he had plenty of "out of college" interns who worked for him. Each one of the latter seemed less and less fluent in the actual English language, and more and more adept at the language of the hip-hop generation. He knew what "waste him" meant. They planned to kill this man. Killing was not what heroes did. He now knew who fought on which side.

Before the hooded figures could produce their weapons, Thesaurus Rex attacked. With his long legs, he could cover three city blocks in less than five seconds. He strode up to the hooded men and head-butted three of them away from the caped man.

The element of surprise was still with him, even after the initial attack. This could be because the assailants were amazed by his size, or the fact that they were looking at something they had thought to be dead for millions of years. Thesaurus Rex took the moment and used it to his advantage. He tail-whipped the two remaining hooded figures who stood behind him. Then he turned his attention to the leader of the group. The saurian champion grabbed the man by sinking his large teeth into the back of his hood, being careful not to actually cause him any.

The hooded figure was terrified. The terror awoke him from his sudden stupor. He reclaimed a grip on his gun and discharged it right into the bottom jaw of the beast.

The gunshot was far more surprising than it was painful to Thesaurus. It hurt like a bee sting, but despite the close proximity of the shot, it did not break his skin. Dr. Adne was right about his bullet-proof scaly skin.

The surprise of the shot caused Thesaurus to open his mouth just wide enough to drop the hooded man. The man fell to the ground in a heap but quickly found purchase on the concrete. Leaving many of his own men behind, he ran and put as much distance as he could between himself and the beast.

54

Thesaurus allowed the man to run. He returned his attention to the men left behind. Those who were earlier head-butted regained consciousness and followed their "fearless" leader. Those who were tail-whipped remained unconscious on the pavement.

Thesaurus left them there and returned his attention to the battered, caped figure. He nudged him with his snout to try to awaken the man. After a second or two, the man regained consciousness.

"Atlas, is that you?" the caped man asked before looking. "Oh geez!" shouted the man as he looked upon Thesaurus Rex.

He quickly stumbled to his feet and postured himself into a fighting stance. By now, Thesaurus was used to reactions such as this. He combated it with his now cliché remark: "Helper, assistant, friend."

The Human Dictionary looked queerly at the dinosaur. "I must have suffered a concussion," he said. "Did you just speak? For that fact, are you even real?"

Thesaurus Rex nodded his head.

HD took a step back and sat down on the curb. He looked at the two unconscious hooded figures still lying on the pavement, then back up at Thesaurus. "You did this?"

Again, the dinosaur nodded his head. The Human Dictionary didn't know what to say.

"Thank you," he finally said. "I would be dead without you."

Thesaurus did not want to nod his head in approval this time; it just seemed too vain. Instead, he smiled at the caped man.

Just then, another man quickly ran around the corner. He was wearing a hood and had a satchel on his back.

"HD! Are you all right?" he called. Suddenly, the new arrival caught a glimpse of the real- life dinosaur standing in front of him and came to a complete stop. "Whoa!"

"It's okay, Atlas. He's an ally," said the Human Dictionary. "He saved me from the Wu Slang Clan."

"Umm... okay?" questioned Atlas. He figured that it didn't quite matter if he was a friend or not. Atlas's lack of fighting skills were no match for the beast in front of him. He then returned his attention to his friend. "Why were you fighting those guys anyway?"

"I didn't plan on fighting them," HD replied. "I was stalking them. I had followed them from the city docks to this point. I was trying to discover their hideout. I suspect it's one of the abandoned buildings around here. I think I know which one, but I'm in no shape to find out for certain."

"So, what happened?"

"Years of martial arts training have molded me into a superior fighter, but they did not mold me into a stealthy fighter. About half a block back, I clumsily stumbled on a sewer grate and knocked over a public trash can. It was like ringing a dinner bell for sharks. They were on me in a heartbeat."

"Did you fight back?"

"Just like last time. They began speaking, and I got weak. I have been trying to train so this wouldn't happen, but it doesn't seem to have worked. Next thing I know, I'm being nuzzled by a should-be-extinct dinosaur." The Human Dictionary pointed at Thesaurus Rex. "How did you know where I was anyway?" HD queried to Atlas.

Atlas reached into his satchel of maps and produced a police scanner. "Blue light special at the Gadget Shack. Friend of mine told me about it."

"Well done," HD commented. "You'll make a decent hero yet. Let's clean up the mess here." He pointed to Thesaurus. "Again, friend, thank you. I will forever be indebted to you. We can take care of these two. I don't think the authorities will take kindly to a loose dinosaur dropping off criminals at the police station."

Thesaurus once again nodded his head. "Agreed, confirmed, concur."

"Where can we call upon you if we need you again?" asked HD.

"Zoo, preserve, sanctuary," Thesaurus said.

"That's right," the Human Dictionary replied. "I remember hearing about a dinosaur taking residence at the zoo. Thank you again, friend. Until we meet again."

With these words, Thesaurus Rex turned and slyly headed back to the zoo.

56

"Atlas, do you mind wrangling these two to the police station? I have a raging headache."

"Sure. Bringing in criminals will help build my street cred," Atlas said as he grouped the collared men.

"Ah," the Human Dictionary said as he momentarily winced in pain.

"What's up, HD?" asked Atlas.

"Cred? Can you be a little more... formal?"

"Sorry, I forgot. Bringing in these guys will raise my credibility."

"That's much better," HD said in relief.

The two men parted ways, never once realizing that their final transaction was being watched *periodically*.

CHAPTER THIRTEEN: Magazine and Clip(ping)

The two henchmen sat down outside the apartment complex where their new "boss" told them to meet. Josh, or Clip(ping) as he was now referred to, sat on the brick fence that lined the apartment complex. He look bewildered. When Heathcliff, or Magazine, noticed the look, he grew annoyed and barked at him.

"What's wrong now?" Magazine asked.

"Last night... you saw the same thing I did, right? The Human Dictionary isn't working alone!"

"Yea, so what? He's got some globe-faced, purse-wearing friend who seems to follow him like a lost puppy. What about it?"

"I don't care about him. I'm talking about the living, talking dinosaur that he has."

"Yeah, that caught me off guard too. But what do you care? With the firepower we have, we could take down an elephant. Heck! We could take down three!"

Clip(ping) just looked down at the cracked sidewalk. "Is this too much?" he asked. "I think that we, or at least I, made a big mistake. Don't get me wrong. We've been friends for a long time, and you know that I want to be a super... hero or villain as much as the next fanboy, but this is way over us. I mean, definition-speaking super humans I can take, but dinosaurs? I think I want out!"

Magazine looked at his friend. The malignant glare he tossed at his friend was strong enough to peel old wallpaper off bad drywall.

"Out? You want out? We've been on one -- *one* -- reconnaissance mission! I don't even think that we've been around long enough to be considered 'in!' And you want out?"

"Heathcliff—"

"Don't call me that! Not anymore! Heathcliff was a powerless dweeb who lived in his parents' basement for too long and could never get out. No one feared Heathcliff. But side-by-side with Lexi Con, Magazine will be feared by the world!"

"Could never get out? What are you talking about? You went away to college for a semester before you decided it would be easier to just commute."

Magazine grew quiet. He lowered his head and took a deep breath. Clip(ping) could see the stress figuratively radiating out of his friend.

"That's not true. That was all a lie," Magazine whispered.

"What are you talking about?"

"Going away to college was the lie that my parents and I came up with to hide the truth from you and the rest of the town. When I left, I didn't go to college. I went to prison."

"What are you talking about?"

Magazine took a deep breath. "Look, Josh... I mean, Clip(ping)... we have been friends forever, but I made some stupid choices. One night, while surfing the web, I was able to successfully hack into one of the largest entertainment conglomerates in the world." Magazine pantomimed with his hands to signal a clear identification for Clip(ping).

"You mean D—"

"Yes, them. And don't say their name. They are so *sue*-happy, they may come after you if you don't have the proper clearance to use it. Plus, I still have a couple of restraining orders against me. But I hacked them."

Clip(ping) looked at his friend with a mixed mask of surprise and respect. "I never knew you were that good of a hacker."

"I wasn't. It took them less than ten minutes to realize the security breach and less time than that to find me. Although I was only able to breach the system for a few minutes, they swore that I'd seen too much, swore that I'd uncovered secrets of upcoming projects; and they feared that I would sell the intelligence to a competitor. Even though I didn't see anything!

"In depositions they pushed for maximum piracy legislation and tried to send me away until the day that the sun sets forever. Thankfully, we were able to reach a plea bargain where they retain the right to sue me until the day I die as long as I spent some time at a minimum security detention facility. It was horrible. It was like a summer camp!"

"How did you hide this from me? I would have understood. This is awesome!"

"I don't know. I guess I was embarrassed. But in those few weeks that I was there, I saw what the real world looks like. It's not all video games and energy drinks. No, it's manual labor and forced exercise! I'm telling you, Clip(ping), I've been to the real world, and I'm not going back. That's why I'm sticking around with Lexi Con. If you look into her eyes, you can tell she has no plans of going there either."

For the first time since this whole thing started, Clip(ping) felt he finally grasped it all. He knew why his friend was all in on this, and now he felt that he was too.

"Ok, I'm in, dinosaur or not. I'm not a Lone Ranger! I'm part of a Dynamic Duo! And you need two for one of those!"

Just then, a flash of purple poly-cotton blend washed past the boys and grabbed them by the ears. "If you two princesses are done playing dress-up now, I need to know what you found out last night so that I can put together a plan."

Lexi Con dragged the two into one of the apartments.

CHAPTER FOURTEEN: Wu Slang Clan

In an abandoned warehouse on the outskirts of town…

"Yo, this is whacked! That stocking-wearing, talking book blew down Spaz and Loke! You gots to do sumthin about this, brah!" a member of the Clan said to the leader.

Despite his many years of street talk, the leader swore that at times his comrades created their own words when they couldn't find the right words to say.

"It's more than that, Homez," another member spat out. "That boy be travelin' wid some wild characters. My boy gots hisself a big lizard and a brotha wearin' a mask! I'm tellin' you this is whack, yo!"

The leader of the Wu Slang Clan sat back in a high barstool he had stolen from the closed coffee shop next door. He couldn't ignore the obvious much longer. This definition-speaking vigilante was becoming an extreme nuisance. It all started with him showing up with his man-purse-wearing friend at the Dino's Diamonds robbery. He still didn't understand how that bullet he got off didn't find its mark.

"Yo, fool, you even listnin' to me? We got to take out that Dictionary dude. I think yous afraid to fight him. If you's too afraid, I can do it for ya."

The leader stood up without ever changing his facial expression. His dark outfit rippled as the loose garment spread out. "Me bein quiet ain't got nothing to do with fear. I ain't afraid of nobody. Not him, and you best be believin I ain't afraid of you neither."

The Clan member tapped his chin as if he were considering how to respond. When he approached his leader, he leaned in closely to whisper to his general.

"If you ain't afraid of me, maybe you should be."

The leader leaned back to look his subordinate in the face. He wasn't stunned about this attempted mutiny. Mutiny among thieves was commonplace. What he was surprised, or more angered, with was this fool's lack of respect.

"You know how I came to be the leader? I whooped everyone else in a rumble. And that includes your sorry butt, brah. Don't be trippin."

The subordinate leaned back with a laugh. "You may have won, but you ain't whoop nobody. You got lucky, and there's no ways that yous could do it again."

"That a fact?"

"Sure 'nough is. How about weez go again. Right here, right now. Winner takes over the Clan. And when I win, I'll get the brothas together to mess up that Dictionary fool."

The leader took a step back and looked over his challenger. His opponent had about an inch and fifty pounds on him, but size was nothing if you didn't know what to do with it. And this fool didn't.

"Your funeral," the leader said as he assumed a fighting stance.

The challenger stepped back and giggled with amusement. In a mocking tone he repeated back, "That a fact?" With a lunge toward his superior, the insubordinate made the first move.

It was a power move engineered to end the fight quickly -- a spear to the sternum. But the leader had been anticipating the move. It had become the challenger's signature attack. The leader quickly moved out of the way and let his adversary run right past him toward the brick wall.

The human bullet was able to slow his momentum before he hit the barrier, but not his posture. The leader slammed his foot into the other's rear, causing his head to make a violent impact into the wall. When the challenger stood, a stream of blood, originating from a gash on his forehead, ran down his face.

"Nice move, but now you done!"

The opponent picked up a loose brick from the floor and hurled it at his adversary. The leader was able to quickly duck under the projectile but was too distracted to pay attention to the follow-up attack as a fist was shoved into his face.

The leader staggered back. He could taste the tang of blood as it trickled down his throat. He knew he was busted open, and it angered him some more. The powerhouse challenger tried to take advantage of his stunned opponent and once again attempted the spear.

Once again, the leader was ready for it. He stepped aside but caught his opponent's face in a head lock. The leader pushed down with all of his weight, slowly closing off the challenger's windpipe.

"You challenged me in my own lair, you called me a coward, and then you attack me," he whispered so that only the insubordinate could hear him. "I told you, it's your funeral!"

With that, the leader rotated his arms. A loud, sickening crack echoed throughout the room, and the insubordinate's body fell limp.

The leader looked out to those who watched the battle. "I'm done with this fool! Let y'all learn not to mess wid me. Get his sorry behind out of here and call the boys in!"

Another subordinate stepped forward in a much more respectful manner. "Which boys you want?"

"Alla them! Shawty, Splintz, Chesta -- all of them. And I want them here no later than tomorrow. We need to plan how we can take down this Human Dictionary fool!"

CHAPTER FIFTEEN: Lexi Con

When a plan comes together, there is no better feeling in the world. It had taken her almost three months of scouting and planning to formulate her plan, but once the chips started falling into place, she could see that it would succeed.

"All right, one last time. Here is the plan to destroy the Human Dictionary," she said to her underlings Magazine and Clip(ping). "Setting a good trap is like landing the big fish. First, you need to present bait too tantalizing to refuse..."

Webster Middle School

"Please excuse the interruption," the principal's voice blurted over a PA speaker throughout the school's campus. "I have a very special announcement! It seems that Webster Middle School has been chosen as the site of a new academic game show! The show is called *Dictionary Bee*! The game is a bee competition about the definitions of everyday words. Our students will be the first contestants of the game. All contestants are guaranteed to be on television. The winner gets a special prize!"

In the middle school geography class

Michael Allen Philips stood at his desk listening to the PA announcement as he unfurled a poster that was sent to him from the school board. On the poster was a picture of the Human Dictionary and a caption that read: "You can be a hero too if you stay in school." As cheesy as the poster was, he felt a pang of jealousy for his new comrade.

As the principal's announcement about the Dictionary Bee trailed off, a hand rose in the back of Mr. Philips's class. "A special prize?" A young girl's voice interrupted Mike's thoughts. "Excuse me, Mr. Philips, do you know what the special prize is?"

64

"Um, no, I do not know, Ariel. I'm sure that if you ask the principal later, he'll know," Mr. Philips responded with a feeling of intrigue. Why hadn't he heard about this Dictionary Bee before?

At a City Bank

"Thanks again, HD," a police officer said as he shook the superhero's hand.

"Always glad to help," the Human Dictionary replied as he watched yet another criminal he assisted in apprehending being placed in the back of the squad car. As was almost tradition at this point, a myriad of media personnel approached him to ask him questions. During the interrogation, a man came toward him wearing a used cotton-polyester blend suit -- because it just breathed better -- and a straw hat with a red, white, and blue ribbon wrapped around it. The man looked like he should be standing on top of a bandstand in a country fair rather than at the scene of a crime.

"Mr. Dictionary, sir," he opened with, "my name is Heathcliff Magazine. I'm the new host of the school game show *Dictionary Bee*. We have a show that is going to take place soon at Webster Middle School right here in the city. We at the game show were wondering if you could honor us as a special guest?"

It's hard for most people to reject such an offer. It's even more difficult to reject it in front of a slew of reporters like the Human Dictionary was. But it's only difficult if it's something you don't want to do.

"I would be delighted to make an appearance," answered the caped hero.

Webster Middle School

"Ladies and gentlemen, boys and girls, welcome to the first ever episode of *Dictionary Bee*!" shouted Heathcliff Magazine in a dramatic voice as the lights in the school auditorium faded and the lights on stage brightened. "Please give a warm round of applause for our contestants."

The emcee pointed to the stage where a group of students sat on small plastic chairs. Each one had a silly paper star with a number pinned to his or her chest. At the end of the row sat a girl with brown curly hair: Ari.

"Now, please help me introduce our special guest: The Human Dictionary!"

The crowd of adolescent admirers began cheering as if a teen pop-singing celebrity was just introduced. From a side door entered the Human Dictionary. The cheers rose to a deafening capacity. Chants of "HD, HD!" rang out through the crowd.

The Human Dictionary waved to his admiring public and was escorted to his special seat in the front of the auditorium. A mass of students was positioned in the auditorium seats while the students participating in the game show sat on stage, nervously awaiting the start of the show.

In the back of the auditorium, Mr. Philips, the geography teacher (or Atlas, as he was known), just smiled and shook his head. Jealousy ran through him at the sight of what his friend was going through.

The Human Dictionary turned around and took his seat just in time to see a masked man wearing a used, cotton-polyester blend suit and holding an automatic weapon in front of him. HD quickly turned to see a man wearing a not-so-nice suit and mask holding another automatic weapon at the back of the auditorium near the exits.

"Everybody quiet down!" cried the armed masked man on stage.

Sitting at the podium on a fake game show set with the other five student contestants was Ari. She began to weep in fear, wishing that her 'Dr. Friend' were here to keep her safe.

"I am Magazine, one half of the Periodicals. Let me introduce my associate, 'Clip,'" he said as he motioned to the gunman at the back of the auditorium. The second gunman grinned.

"A Clip is not a periodical!" some wise-mouthed student cried out from the mass.

"It's short for Clipping. Any more comments from the Peanut Gallery and we can see what else we can shorten around here!"

cried Clip. "Like the population!" Clip smiled to himself for the well-delivered pun.

"It seems that your game show has been canceled, but you're in luck," said Magazine. "We have a new guest speaker to occupy your time. Now let me introduce the real star of the show. She is the *definition* of evil. In a world where information is power, she is the queen. She is Lexi Con!"

Suddenly, a woman wearing a purple and black, cotton-polyester blend unitard with the letters "LC" emblazoned on the front was lowered down from a catwalk. Lexi thought about rewarding Magazine later for such an introduction.

The Human Dictionary then realized that he had willingly walked right into a trap, and he had no idea how he could work himself out of it. The last time he had spoken to Lexi was just before his accident. He had no clue what she was capable of or why she was even acting this way and he was quite confused. But he knew that he needed to find out what she was up to -- and fast.

CHAPTER SIXTEEN: Thesaurus Rex

The City Zoo

Dr. Adne shut the door behind him. He dressed himself in scrubs, donned a face mask, and scrubbed his hands with soap and water up to his arms. He was preparing to perform a C-section delivery on a pregnant lioness. Unfortunately, he had an audience. The new holding pen for Thesaurus Rex had not yet been completed, so the dinosaur still maintained residence in the quarantine section of the park where most animal surgeries took place.

An interesting change was taking place inside of Thesaurus Rex. Since his birth -- or rebirth -- he had always had the animal sensations of the dinosaur he was. But he still could feel the humanity inside his mind. Lately, it seemed that that humanity was ebbing away, and more and more of those animal instincts were taking over. For instance, as he watched the surgery, all Thesaurus Rex could think about was how tasty the sleeping lioness looked.

Suddenly, a phone began to ring. Dr. Adne looked down at the cell phone hanging from his belt buckle. The phone played the melody to the popular song "The Lion Sleeps Tonight." Dr. Adne laughed to himself over the irony of the moment.

"That's Ari's mom's ringtone," he said aloud. "I told her not to call me today."

The phone stopped ringing. Seconds later, it began to ring again. Just like the first time, Dr. Adne ignored the musical tone and tried to concentrate on his work. A few seconds later, a tubular tone announced that a voice mail had been left behind.

Dr. Adne looked up from his work and over to the other side of the room where the former doctor, the once human Thesaurus Rex, chewed on what appeared to be a wildebeest leg hanging from the side of his mouth. The zoo had recently allowed their newest resident to enjoy the remains of their late residents who passed due to old age.

"Women!" Dr. Adne spoke to the dinosaur.

Although when he was human Dr. O'Nim had very little interaction with anyone from the opposite gender, the cliché spoke idiomatic volumes to the beast.

Moments later, the phone in the quarantine pen began to ring.

Dr. Adne looked up from the lioness again. "Are you kidding me?"

Just like the cell phone, Dr. Adne ignored the ringing distraction. "Does anyone understand what the term 'no calls' means?"

The scientist nevertheless managed to successfully deliver the new baby cubs. It was a litter of four: three males and one female. The new kings and queen of the jungle took in their new surroundings. They understood, despite their titles, they were kings and queen of nothing as long as Thesaurus Rex was nearby.

Dr. Adne finished up with the mother. He made the determination that she would successfully recover from the procedure. He set her up with an antibiotic drip to fight off any infection that might try to fight its way in, and he finally turned his attention to the missed calls on his cell phone.

With his enhanced audio capacity, Thesaurus Rex could hear the messages as if he himself held the phone to his head.

"First new message," a British-sounding female voice spoke.

"Roger! Roger, where are you! Why aren't you picking up?"

Dr. Adne shook his head. He played with his phone to delete the new message and go on to the next one. As he did this, he spoke again to Thesaurus Rex. "I love it when she does that. Does she expect my voice mail to answer the question?" He laughed and shook his head.

"Next new message."

"Roger! Roger! Our daughter! Oh God!" Ari's mother shouted over the phone.   "Turn on Channel Six News when you get this message and call me now!"

At the news that something may have been wrong with his daughter, Dr. Adne dropped the bemused attitude and ran to the television sitting on the desk in the office next to the quarantine pen.

Dr. Adne began switching the channel before the set had a chance to fully warm up. A voice began to speak over the set before the picture came on the screen:

"Breaking News from News Copter Six. It seems that a team of gun-toting villains has taken over Webster Middle School under the guise of a game show crew. They have taken the entire student body and faculty as hostages. No demands have been made as of yet, but police are trying to make contact with the terrorists."

"Oh, my God!" Dr. Adne shouted. "That's Ari's school. She was supposed to be on that game show today!"

Dr. Adne picked up his phone and returned his wife's call. When it connected, a busy signal shrieked through the receiver. *She must be trying to call the school*, he thought.

As he hung up the phone, the scientist turned to break the news to Ari's best friend. Instead, the doctor found himself standing alone in the quarantine pen with a few lion cubs, a sedated lioness, and a wide open receiving bay door large enough for a dinosaur to walk through.

"This just in to News Copter Six. Reports are coming in that the Human Dictionary is already on the scene, and -- holy cow! Jerry, take us over there! Is that a dinosaur?"

In the City Streets

Although he had no idea where her school was, Thesaurus Rex's sense of smell was just as heightened as his sense of hearing. The second he walked out of the zoo, he picked up her scent.

He knew that he should have had someone alert the proper authorities before leaving the zoo, but this was Ari. She needed his help, and he was on his way.

Despite the rule-breaking, all the people that he ran past didn't seem to fear him; rather, they seemed to cheer him. Slowly, the cheers were drowned out by the rhythmic chopping of helicopter blades from above. That sound dissipated the closer he got to Ari's scent because of the deafening roar of the police car sirens outside the school.

CHAPTER SEVENTEEN: Atlas

There are people who joke about that moment when their worst nightmare becomes true. For Michael A. Philips, that moment actually happened the moment a crew member of a supposed educational game show donned a mask and pulled out an automatic machine gun the size of a trombone.

All that he could think about was the statement made by his defense class instructor if such a situation were to occur: *"Disable your attacker, run to the busiest street corner, then, at the top of your lungs, call for the Human Dictionary; he should be able to help you."* He looked to the front of the auditorium where HD currently sat with guns trained on him. *Little help there*, Michael thought.

The terrified screams of his students snapped Michael's attention back to the situation at hand. He understood that his main objective right then wasn't to engage the armed intruder in combat, but rather to ensure the safety of his students. His fighting skills (or lack thereof) would prove useless in this situation. At best, if he fought the gunman, he would probably put his students in greater risk of danger.

They didn't need a hero right then. What they needed was a teacher. And not a fighter. They needed *a thinker*.

This new thought made Michael relax some. Fighting was not his forte, but thinking was something he was pretty good at. He knew he had to draw the gunman's attention away from the students.

Quicker than any physical action he could have mustered, Michael developed a plan.

He observed that he was standing next to the emergency doors. The doors remained locked at all times to keep intruders out and truants in; but if an emergency alarm were to be tripped, they would open automatically.

He quickly ran to the locked emergency door and shook it, knowing it wouldn't open. He looked terrified. Sweat began to bead on his forehead, and his arms and legs began to tremble as he stared at the gunman.

"Cut that out!" ordered the terrorist.

Michael did not respond verbally. All he could do was shake the doors even harder and louder. This drew the gunman's attention away from the students and back on Michael.

The gunman, Clip(ping), approached him. Mike began to curl up on the floor and weep, "Please don't hurt me! I won't try to stop you; I just want to go home."

"Doesn't work that way! You came here to see a show and boy do we have one planned for you! Now get up!"

Michael remained in a curled ball next to the locked doors. He refused to move.

"I said get up!" Clip cried as he kicked Michael.

Michael sprang to his feet and then stayed put. He looked completely helpless and terrified.

Clip approached the teacher, grabbed his arms, turned him around, and pushed him toward the seats. "Now sit down before you miss all the fun!"

Fighting was obviously not a talent that Michael possessed. Thinking was something he was better at. But apparently, acting was where all of his talent lay. The prostrate façade that Michael created fooled the slow-witted Clip into a sense of false security. The gunman let down his guard and placed himself in the exact position Michael wanted him to be in.

"Ok, just please don't hurt me. This was what I was looking for," Michael said to Clip.

"What? A seat?" questioned the gunman.

"No, a *SIGN!*" Michael shouted.

Before Clip could even understand the statement, Michael A. Phillips the thinker and actor became Mike the fighter. He quickly jabbed his sharp elbow into the sternum of the gunman, promptly knocking the wind out of him.

"S!" Mike shouted.

Next, before Clip had a chance to realize what was going on and react to it, Mike slammed his heel into his opponent's instep with a bone-chilling crack.

"I!"

As Clip grabbed his foot to cry in pain, Mike turned and hit the gunman where no man should ever hit another.

"G!" he sang out.

And lastly, as the former fake crew member leaned forward in immense pain, Mike balled his fists and struck the man in the bridge of his nose with another sickening crunch.

"N!"

Clip lay on the floor unmoving, either unconscious or too embarrassed to get up.

It appeared that the darkness at the back of the auditorium had assisted Mike. The gunman Magazine and his female boss on stage did not seem to notice any of the action that took place there.

Michael took advantage of this darkness once again. He quickly began to usher out as many students as he could from the auditorium. Once he got them to safety, he made his way to his classroom and got into his closet.

Hanging off the back of his closet was the leather jacket with the dark yellow mustard stain on the sleeve that he wore to school that morning. On the hook next to the outerwear was a beige, torn satchel holding a number of maps in canisters and a mask that looked like a globe.

A hero was what they needed right now. And for the first time ever, he felt like that hero.

CHAPTER EIGHTEEN: The Human Dictionary

For months now he had been ridding the city streets from the vermin that crawled underneath it. In all that time, he never once heard of these Periodicals or their feminine leader, Lexi Con. In a matter of minutes, these three villains had outsmarted him. Worst of all, he had placed the children (and their education) in peril.

Despite all of the terrible things that had happened, HD could not help but think that this new enemy, this Lexi Con, seemed familiar. Was she the reincarnation of a past antagonist? Even after some thought, he still couldn't place where he had seen this woman before.

"What's wrong, Human Dictionary? Cat got your tongue?" Lexi said, her fists clenched.

"Despite your disrespect to the educational value of game shows, I can see that you still respect the value of an idiom or cliché," he bantered back.

"Cliché. Noun: a trite, stereotyped expression; a sentence or phrase, usually expressing a popular or common thought or idea," she spat back at the Human Dictionary.

HD stared at Lexi in disbelief. Just as quickly as he recalled the definition, she had shot it right back at him. How was this possible?

"What's wrong now? Did you think you had the market cornered on literary superpowers?"

HD was speechless. What was the point in speaking? Speaking used to be his one true power. It was his power to inform, his power to distract, his power *alone*. But what was the point to using it when it could just as quickly be spat back at you? This was worse than the slang deficiency. When that happened, he was powerless. Powerless he could deal with, but having power that was completely useless -- this was different.

"You never could accept the fact that others were better than you," she said angrily.

"I never could accept...? Do I know you?" the Human Dictionary questioned.

"Typical! You can never see what is right before your eyes. But I think it's time that we fix that problem. Go ahead; take a deep, long look. See for yourself what you helped create."

The Human Dictionary gaped confusedly, but then he saw something. It was something that he hadn't seen in years: a small dimple that he once knew but that seemed changed over time. It had been twisted and gnarled by years of anger, fury, and rage. For the first time, the Human Dictionary stared at who stood before him.

"Lexi? he asked in disbelief. "Is that you?"

"How touching," she jeered at him. "You almost sound like you care about me."

"Lexi, what happened to you? How did this happen?"

"Lexi was the sister you used to tease when you were younger. The girl that you and your friends would drop buckets of water on from the roof just to see how angry she would get. Lexi was the little girl you left behind when you went away to college to be a big man. Well, guess what? Lexi is gone now. All that remains is Lexi Con."

At HD's confusion, Lexi Con snorted. "Don't act like you don't know. I don't know how you did this, Ritchie, but you did. And for once, I appreciate the gift you have given me. More important, I intend for it to be a one-of-a-kind gift."

"How I did it?" He slowly stood from his seat and began to advance toward her. "Do you think that I planned this?" he shouted at his sister. "Lexi, this happened by accident; I never intended for this to happen. I certainly never thought that anything would happen to you!"

"What a shock," she interrupted. "You weren't thinking about me. Well, guess what? I *have* been thinking a lot about you. I have kept a very close eye on you for some time now, and I now know you better than I have ever known you. Better yet, I now know you better than you know yourself."

"What is that supposed to mean?"

"It means that, although you were the genesis of these powers, I have become the master. I have stretched them to their full strength and have tested and eliminated the deficiencies."

"Just because you know all of these big words doesn't mean you need to show off in front of all of these kids."

Lexi began to laugh at her brother's sass. "You're right. I'll just put it in terms that they can better understand. Although you started this power, I have become a queen of it, while you have become a helpless *muggle*."

The Human Dictionary crumpled to the ground. The pain of an informal word began to numb his whole body. She knew the weaknesses of his powers.

He looked up, and his jaw dropped. The pain was excruciating to him, but she didn't even flinch at the use of the word. How could this be? Did she not have the same powers as he did? Shouldn't she have the same weaknesses as well?

"I have to be honest... I just cannot get enough of that facial expression. It has made up for the past few years of bad birthday presents." She laughed.

"How... how are you unaffected by that informal word?" HD meekly asked.

"I can't pretend that I truly understand the phenomenon myself," she said as she approached her brother's limp body on the floor. "I guess it just comes down to the fact that you dictionary types are just a bunch of stuffed shirts that have to remain formal and are too stubborn to accept new words, while we Lexicon types are more accepting of the constant trend of creating new words. Did you know that there are complete lexicons for each sport and computer lingo, *bro*?"

The abbreviated use of the word caused the Human Dictionary to writhe in more pain.

"You see, I have been watching you for some time now. I know all of your secrets. I watched you in that record store as you grew weak listening to those country, rap, and hip-hop albums while you dim-wittedly flirted with that salesgirl."

Lexi began circling around her brother, much like a predator looking for the death blow. "I have to admit, you have dated worse. It only took me a few moments to realize what was bothering you in that store; what made you so ill."

The Human Dictionary very slowly and very painfully set both of his feet on the ground. It was a feat of incredible strength just to move that much. Lexi laughed at the pain he was enduring.

"Once I knew your weakness, it only took me a matter of hours to devise a plan to destroy you. And how easy that was. You were as pompous as ever. And how could you, the white knight for all things grammatically correct, turn down an invitation to an academic game show. Your predictability is truly your worst weakness."

Suddenly, a student sitting near the conversation spoke up. "That's your brother?" he asked. "And you're treating him like that? Man, that's the *fashizzle*."

Simultaneously, both the Human Dictionary and Lexi Con grabbed their temples as skull-cracking headaches erupted inside their heads. As HD tried to regain his composure, he looked over at Lexi Con and saw her struggling with the effects of the slang term as well.

With the quickness of a young cat, an enraged Lexi sprung upon the student and grabbed him by the shoulders. She began to violently shake him and shout, "What does it mean? What does it mean?"

Shocked by the sudden attack, the student tried to explain to the woman the definition of his street talk. "It means 'that's interesting' but in a more profane way," he admitted.

HD knew right away what was going on. Lexi Con could stand the informal words, just so long as she could accept them into her lexicon. Before that, they were as poisonous to her as they were to him. He finally knew her weakness; now he just needed to exploit it. But first things first. He needed to get her away from these kids before she or her slow-witted henchmen could hurt them. This required a distraction, and he looked above the stage to find exactly what he was looking for.

As Lexi Con slackened the grip she had on the young man who enlightened her on a new slang word, she looked over to see her once ailing brother regaining his vertical position as he pulled a small leather pouch from his side pocket.

"What's that?" she queried. "A male purse?"

"No," he replied. "It's my checkbook."

He opened the pouch and pulled out three small steel checkmarks with the letters "abc" engraved across them. He looked up above the stage at the emergency sprinkler system. Lexi Con had flashbacks to all of the times she was doused from above by Ritchie and his friends when they were little. She began to move to pounce on him, but it was too late. He unleashed the throwing stars toward the sprinklers.

A loud clank was followed by an even louder alarm. Bells rang out through the school. The automatically locked emergency doors swung open as water began to pour down on the kids. Using the sudden distraction to their advantage, the remaining teachers began to quickly escort as many students as they could out the doors.

Lexi Con growled louder than a mother grizzly protecting her cubs. All of this planning (and cotton polyester blend) was ruined. She turned her attention back to her brother.

The Human Dictionary knew that the students would be safer now, but he still needed to stop Lexi. The ear-shattering sound of the alarms was not doing his headache any justice. He knew he had to take this fight somewhere else, so he peered through the wide-open emergency doors.

"You still want me? Come and get me then!" he shouted at his sister as he ran toward the sunlight.

CHAPTER NINETEEN: Thesaurus Rex

On the auditorium stage

The sudden alarm, sprinkling water, and mass exodus of hostages took Magazine completely off guard. He turned to see what Lexi Con wanted him to do, but he only caught a glimpse of her as she hurried out the open emergency door into the sunlight. A quick glance to the back of the auditorium proved that Clip(ping) was gone as well.

Magazine was alone. Worse yet, he had no leverage to get past the horde of police officers outside of the emergency doors. That was, until he heard the whimper of the game show contestants who were still on stage.

He didn't want to do this in the first place. It was all Clip(ping)'s idea to hunt down Lexi Con and become henchmen. He just wanted to show off his impressive shooting skills. And he would be damned if anyone thought he was going to jail for this. He knew that it was only a matter of time until the police came barging in and surrounded him. He had played enough video games to know what would happen once the police came in. He also had played enough video games to know how to get out of this situation without being put into a cage again, but he would need protection.

Magazine walked up to the frightened game show contestants. "All right, listen to me, and nobody gets hurt. I need to get out of here, and you six are going to help me. So, get up!"

None of the contestants moved a muscle. Afraid that at any moment the police were going to storm in, Magazine reached out and grabbed the girl with dark brown, curly hair. "You are going to be my human shield. Stand in front of me and protect me from the cop's bullets. The rest of you, if you don't want to see your friend get shot by me, better get up and join her."

The other five were terrified. Regardless of the terror experienced by them, they couldn't just sit and watch their friend get murdered. They slowly rose and circled around the gunman.

"Nice and slow now. As a group, we are going to walk outside. Keep in mind, if you six stay around me, I probably won't go to jail. If one of you runs off, it would be as if all of you ran off; I would be exposed. That said, anyone runs, I start shooting. Understand?"

Through the sounds of weeping and sobs, the six former contestants answered in agreement. Together, they began to walk outside.

Outside the school

It was an unusual scene when Thesaurus Rex first arrived. A few police officers in full riot gear ran out with loaded weapons to greet him. Only after the commissioner himself ordered their guns to be lowered did any of them react. After the commissioner vouched for Thesaurus Rex's safety and trust, not a single officer even gave him a dirty look.

Despite being a large beast, Thesaurus Rex still partly maintained the mind of a genius. As he stood outside the school, he could assess the events that were going on inside, thanks to his enhanced senses. He understood that if he charged into the school, he would only complicate the situation further.

Students would not be expecting a dinosaur to come in. Such a strange occurrence would cause pandemonium. That could lead to people getting hurt, which in turn could lead to Ari getting hurt. That was what he was here to prevent.

Suddenly, a loud alarm went off and the emergency doors swung open. By the sound, Thesaurus Rex assumed that a fire alarm had gone off. Using his keen sense of smell, he ruled out an actual fire.

Many students quickly exited the building. Even with hundreds of kids piling out, Thesaurus Rex knew that Ari had not come out. The same sweet scent that he traced to this school seemed strangely absent. Ari was still in the building.

Then, there was a quick flash that T-Rex caught out of the corner of his eye. When he turned his attention to it, he saw the man he met the other night, the Human Dictionary, standing next to a fallen trash can. He then ran down the street with a mysterious masked woman chasing after him.

Thesaurus thought about pursuing them but decided against it. HD was free for now. Ari, on the other hand, may still need his help.

No sooner had this thought crossed his mind when he saw her. It was just as he feared. There was his curly brown-haired friend with an automatic rifle pushed between her shoulder blades.

At that moment, something snapped inside the mind of Thesaurus Rex. The part of his brain that thought at a human level hibernated for a few moments, and the animal instincts that had been overruling his brain kicked into high gear once again.

The police, seeing that the gunman had surrounded himself with hostages, made no advance to try and stop him. Suddenly, like a blur, a giant dinosaur barreled down upon the group.

Magazine did not see the beast charging at first, and when he finally did realize what was going on, he was too horrified to react. This helped Thesaurus Rex close some ground.

As he had originally predicted, the sight of a giant dinosaur made the students react. The game show contestants feared being shot, but apparently not as much as they feared being eaten by a dinosaur.

Thesaurus Rex knew what would happen if the kids ran. He heard what the gunman had said to them inside. He shouted at them to stay where they were: "Stop, halt, desist!" His cries, however, fell on deaf ears. As soon as they saw the monster, the kids began to run from the gunman.

Seeing her Dr. Friend, Ari stopped moving and smiled. This was the wrong choice. Realizing that Ari was the only hostage he had left and coming to the conclusion that a supposed extinct monster was closing in on him, Magazine went into survival mode. He began to spray the area with bullets.

There was so much noise that one sound could not be distinguished from another. The police pulled the running hostages to protection. The police officers who weren't near the safety of shelter were the ones still donning bulletproof riot gear from Thesaurus Rex's approach. When it came down to it, the only two targets that were vulnerable to fire were Ari and Thesaurus Rex.

Ari heard the initial shot and closed her eyes. She didn't want to see what was about to happen. Seconds, maybe even less than that, before Magazine pulled the trigger, Thesaurus Rex was able to shield Ari from the gunfire. When Magazine pulled the trigger, he emptied an entire clip into the exposed side of the sentient dinosaur.

At the sound of the rounds finding their target, Ari's eyes whipped open. All she could see of her friend was his massive torso before her. She watched as his chest began to heave and his breaths became deeper and longer. Something wasn't right. She wrapped her arms around her Dr. Friend and wept tears of sorrow, knowing this was the last time he would ever save her.

When the clip finally emptied, Magazine continued to depress the trigger, not realizing that he was out of ammunition. After he let go of the trigger, the clicking sound stopped, and once again silence returned.

Ari pushed on Thesaurus Rex's side and urged the giant behemoth to move, to show some sign of life. Nothing happened.

Magazine stood in awe of everything that had just happened in front of him. A monster survived millions of years of extinction just to be killed by him. In a state of mixed emotions and confusion, he dropped his weapon.

Before the gun even struck the ground, Magazine was upended. A swirling blue line came up from behind him and knocked him unconscious. Thesaurus Rex's tail took out the last threat in the school yard. Then he stood up from the crouched position that he maintained until he knew that Ari was completely out of harm's way.

On the ground next to his body were the rounds of the automatic weapon with flattened heads. Thesaurus Rex's iron-like scales survived the onslaught. Although he had lost a scale or two and was bleeding in some spots, his most vital organ, his heart -- Ari -- was fine.

CHAPTER TWENTY: The Human Dictionary

As the Human Dictionary broke out into the bright sunlight, his senses were assaulted by a memory… he had been here before. He ran past a battalion of police officers and began to slow. Why was this place so familiar? Then he saw something. He ran up next to it and stopped.

A million things were out of place at the moment, none more obvious than a million-year-old dinosaur standing in a schoolyard. But the item that caught the Human Dictionary's attention was an upended trash can. He wasn't so concerned about how it became overturned. Truth was that he knew that he had done it. What caught his attention the most was an understanding of where he was. The costumed hero looked up at the surrounding buildings, then back at the form of his approaching sister. He devised a plan and took off toward the buildings.

As he ran, he could hear Lexi screaming in anger. He knew she would be angry. His quick thinking and speedy reactions not only ruined her plans to kidnap him, but he had also removed her from her school full of hostages.

The Human Dictionary was gambling on the idea that his sister would be enraged enough to follow him wherever he went. He wasn't quite sure, but he had his suspicions that there might be a place nearby that would level the playing field for the two wordsmiths. If this was going to work, he needed to make sure that Lexi Con was right on him. If he distanced himself too far from her, this plan could backfire in a hurry. He slyly slowed down, but not to the extent that would be obvious to Lexi Con.

Lexi Con began to close the distance between herself and the Human Dictionary. The latter could hear her heavy breaths as she got closer and closer. He wasn't certain if her exhalations were so deep because she was out of breath from running or from seething with anger. Either way, he knew that he needed to end this foot race soon.

HD finally saw the target he was looking for: a large, frosted window with a picture of a steaming cup of coffee on the front of a supposedly abandoned building -- a former coffee café in the heart of the industrial park. He ran in front of the window and came to a screeching halt. If he knew his sister, he knew that she would not do the same. Her rage would catapult them both through the window. As she got closer, he used the only defense he could: he put his fingers in his ears and began to chant gibberish.

Just as the Human Dictionary had predicted, Lexi Con pounced on her brother and drove them both into the pane glass. The force of their impact caused the transparent substance to shatter and splinter. Shards of the glass dug into the back of the Human Dictionary while fragments stuck in Lexi Con's hair. The struggle caused so much noise that it disturbed the meeting taking place on the other side of the window.

Exploiting someone's weakness is the best way to stop him or her. But what do you do when their only weakness is your only weakness too? The Human Dictionary realized the answer to that one was the classic idiom: take one for the team.

As the glass shattered around the warring siblings, they fell to the floor of the secret hub of the nefarious Wu Slang Clan.

The Human Dictionary had been spying on the gang for weeks and had surmised that this was their hiding place. He realized that the fallen trash can outside the school was the very same one he had stumbled over the other night when he was tracking a small cell of the group. Anticipating the verbal barrage of slang words the gang would assault them with after they came through the window, the Human Dictionary tried to cover his ears to protect himself.

"What the—? Yo, it's the po-po!" one of them shouted.

"Nah brah, it's the stupid caped playa that's been followin' us. Looks like he brought a pigeon wit' him."

"Yo baby, what's crackalackin'?"

Lexi Con's mind started to numb and go white with pain. She quickly jumped on the last gangster who spoke and began to assault him, trying to bleed from him the information that she needed to stop the pain. Meanwhile, the Human Dictionary was sprawled out in a pile of broken glass with his fingers in his ears as he sang "The Alphabet Song."

"What does it mean?" Lexi Con shouted at the criminal. "What does it mean!"

"Yo, somebody get this fool offa me!"

"Sugar, don't hate the playa."

"Dis girl be perpetratin'."

With each new slang word used, Lexi Con's strength ebbed away. She attacked a few of the members, but it was only a matter of a few seconds until she was reduced to a limp body on the floor.

"Man, waste this fool and his pigeon before the real po-po come knockin' down our door."

There was a conflict brewing in the Human Dictionary's mind. Although moments ago Lexi Con tried to destroy him, she was still his sister, and nobody was going to hurt her.

When the gangster pulled out his gun, the still-functioning Human Dictionary swirled his body around in the pool of broken window glass he was lying in and took out the gunman's feet. Seconds later, he was being attacked by the remaining gang members, both physically and verbally.

During the attack, HD realized something: his training had made some difference. Although his head was swirling with informal speech, the words that he had previously heard (such as the words in the rap and hip-hop songs) stung far less than the new words.

He defended himself the best he could, but there were just too many of them. He knew coming into this fight that he had no end game. He needed to neutralize Lexi Con, and he had done that. He never planned on how to get both of them out of there.

By his rough calculations, there were about a dozen gang members in the room. Lexi had neutralized three, and he had taken out about half a dozen, but the odds where just not in his favor. He collapsed to the floor in a fit of exhaustion and pain. His breaths were deep and labored; shards of glass were studded throughout his back.

The masked leader of the gang walked up to HD and stared at him. "I'm done wit' you, fool. In the past few weeks, you have had

85

more than half of my peeps in cuffs. Not no more. It's time that I finally waste you."

Holding a semi-automatic handgun, the man raised his arm. HD was too exhausted to move. He closed his eyes.

A loud bang made everything quiet again. The Human Dictionary felt no different than he had seconds before. The exhaustion had not changed; neither had the skull-splitting headache. He felt a little disappointment, thinking that at least in death the pain would go away. Then he heard a similar bang, only this one didn't sound like a gunshot, but rather like a blunt object being crushed into someone's skull.

The Human Dictionary opened his eyes. He wasn't dead and he saw his friend Atlas taking on the remaining gangsters. It seemed that before the gangster could pull the trigger, Atlas hit him across the back, causing his shot to go errant.

HD, being too tired to move at first, watched his friend fight the remaining three gang members. His fighting still was a little off -- it consisted of mostly hitting the goons with his torn satchel and then kicking them in the groin -- but at this point anything worked.

Atlas had neutralized two of the gang members. The third one was starting to get the better of him.

HD mustered all the strength he had and chopped the final assailant across the back of the neck, knocking him unconscious. The threat of the Wu Slang Clan had been neutralized.

"How did you know where I was?" asked the Human Dictionary.

"I just happened to be near the school when all this went down, and so was Thesaurus Rex. He walked over to a fallen trash can and said, 'Evidence, clue, hint.' I recognized the neighborhood from the other night and ran around until I found the broken window." Atlas grinned. "Rough entry?" he joked.

The two men laughed until they heard the unmistakable click of a handgun being cocked. They turned around to see a thirteenth member of the gang emerging from behind the café countertop next to a broken tray that probably used to hold muffins and scones. He pointed his gun at the two heroes. Both men froze.

"You know, for a brotha, you ain't too bright," the gang member said. "Ain't you seen any horror movies? Someone is always in the backroom."

The two men were out of position with their guards down. If either of them tried to advance on the man, it was more likely that he would get a shot off before they got to him. And in these close quarters, it was nearly impossible to miss.

"You don't need to do this, man," Atlas spoke.

In contrast, the Human Dictionary was speechless. He was actually rather shocked that his ally had the ability to speak right then; it always seemed that he himself was more verbose in these dangerous situations while Atlas played the role of the quiet bystander. Things were clearly changing. If he got out of there alive, he was going back to get that record girl's number.

"I don't?" the gunman questioned. "I just saw two of the city's top superheroes and some freaky chick take out a dozen of my brothas, and you don't think I need to do this? Even better, there is a circus of Five-O right down the street. You think I can just walk away from this? Fool, you trippin'."

Neither man could move fast enough. They both pushed to charge, but the gangster was in a better position. He pulled the trigger. There was a loud *pop!*

All three men stared. The bullet was discharged from the gun, and then floated in midair between the three of them.

"How are you doing that?" Atlas asked the Human Dictionary.

"I'm not!" HD responded.

Suddenly, a blinding wind forced through the shattered remains of the window. All of the debris in the room was swept aside. Atlas and the Human Dictionary stared in awe behind the last gangster. There, standing behind him, was an elderly man with long white hair and an even longer white beard. He wore old, tattered garments, and held a staff with what looked like an emerald inlaid atop it.

"I did," said the man.

With nearly blinding speed, the older man whipped his staff across the face of the gangster, knocking him unconscious. The floating bullet fell to the floor.

"Who are you?" both men queried simultaneously.

"I am Encyclone-pedia, master and manipulator of the wind and recorder of facts," the white-haired gentleman replied. "I have been watching you and protecting you for some time. I think it is about time for us and your dinosaur friend to talk."

The two heroes looked at each other with an expression of pure confusion and awe.

"Talk about what?" the Human Dictionary asked.

"Talk about resurrecting *The References*."

EPILOGUE

The City Zoo

Dr. Adne listened intently as the news of the terrorist holdout came over the small television he kept in his office.

"Today at Webster Middle School, a strange turn of events took place. The school was supposed to host a new educational game show, but that appears to have been just a ruse to catch the superhero known as the Human Dictionary. The crew members, later revealed to be a supervillain by the name of Lexi Con and her two henchmen, the Periodicals – individually known as Magazine and Clip -- brandished automatic weapons and held the superhero, the school faculty, and all of the students hostage.

"It seemed that some quick thinking on the part of the Human Dictionary saved the students from the criminals' grasp. When he activated the school fire safety system, the locked doors automatically opened. Teachers quickly escorted the students to safety.

"This day was not without its share of heroes. Not only did the Human Dictionary and Atlas bring Lexi Con, her crew, and , , the criminal masterminds of the gang called the Wu Slang Clan to justice, but in a bizarre, unrelated twist the friendly dinosaur, Thesaurus Rex, risked his own life for the safety of a young girl as he brought the masked gunman Magazine down..

"Additionally, one unlikely unmasked man was truly heroic today. Middle school geography teacher, Michael Allen Philips, took out the gunman Clip in hand-to-hand combat and pulled a number of students to safety. It just goes to show that the real heroes are the everyday people like teachers, cops, and firefighters.

"When all was said and done, nobody was harmed, and all guilty parties were taken into custody. Reporting live from News Copter Six, I am Merriam Roget."

In a prison cell

Weeks of planning had led her there. Despite all the preparations, she was now confined to a cell. That part she could deal with. The part she couldn't was that Ritchie was not only still alive, he was more popular than ever for putting her in here.

"Prison bars cannot hold back my wrath," she said aloud. "I will get out, and he will pay."

Then suddenly, Lexi Con heard something. Someone was listening to her outside her cell window.

"Who's there?" she asked aloud. "Reveal yourself!"

No one responded to her threatening tone.

"You would do well to listen to me," she said as she stood up and walked to the barred window. "I am the *definition* of evil. In a world where information is power, I am a queen—"

Her monologue was cut short. A powerful electrical burst shot off outside her window. Then one arm grabbed the frame and ripped off half of her cell wall to reveal the outside world.

On the other side of the crumpled wall stood a massive figure. He appeared to be part human and part machine. He looked down at Lexi Con and spoke.

"In a world where information is power, I am a god! I am Wicked-pedia, and I could use a henchman like you."

Lexi Con was no one's henchman. She held the spotlight all on her own. But one look at this robotic monster, and she decided she could make the adjustment just this once.

To be continued...

If you enjoyed *The References*, please do not hesitate to let us know with an honest positive review on Amazon, GoodReads, your own blog, etc.! The more good reviews, the more sales we make, and the more awesome material Wild Hunt Press can bring you! Any other comments you want to share about this book, please feel free to look up and join the Wild Hunt Press group and page on Facebook, or write the publisher: wildhuntpress@gmail.com.

ABOUT THE AUTHOR

Mark Dennion is a graduate of Rutgers Camden and is a middle school Reading/Language Arts teacher who has been a fan of comics and heroes for as long as he can remember. He got the idea of *The References* from a project that he assigned his students after watching an episode of *South Park*. *The References* is his debut novel, but he hopes it to be the start of a long career. He lives in New Jersey with his beautiful wife and daughter and is content on only writing about superheroes -- well, at least until he learns some karate!